A King Production presents…

SUPREME

MEN OF THE BITCH SERIES

JOY DEJA KING

Cover concept by Joy Deja King

Library of Congress Cataloging-in-Publication Data;
King, Deja Joy

Supreme: Men Of The Bitch Series a series/by Joy Deja King
For complete Library of Congress Copyright info visit:

www.joydejaking.com Twitter: @joydejaking

A King Production
P.O. Box 912, Collierville, TN 38027

A King Production and the above portrayal logo are trademarks of A King Production LLC.

They Don't Paint Pictures They Just Trace Me...

Jay Z

This Book is Dedicated To My:

Family, Readers and Supporters.
I LOVE you guys so much. Please believe that!!

A KING PRODUCTION

SUPREME

MEN OF THE BITCH SERIES

JOY DEJA KING

Chapter One

I Will Be King

From my very first recollection as a kid, I remember staring my parents directly in their eyes while sitting at the dinner table and stating without hesitation, "I will be king." I then looked back down at my plate of food and continued to eat.

"Xavier, what did you say?" my mother questioned, seeming completely bewildered by my comment.

"I said, I'll be king," I repeated, shrugging my shoulders in a nonchalant way. Even then at the age of four or five I had this I don't give a fuck aura about myself. When I was younger, people mistook it as me being disengaged from others. When I got older, people labeled me as arrogant, but honestly it was none of the above. I just knew, I always knew, that I would be somebody great, that I would leave a legacy that my children and grandchildren would admire and respect.

"Boy, what are you talking about now?" My dad chuckled, glancing over at my mother. "You always talking crazy. I tell you what you gon' be… a damn comedian." He laughed. My dad didn't mean any harm, he just didn't know any better.

I didn't even respond to my dad. Once again I shrugged my shoulders and continued eating my dinner. At that time, I wasn't sure the path in life I would take that would make me king. I was only sure that greatness awaited me and I was looking forward to taking my spot on the throne.

"Only one more week of school and then summer vacation… yes!" I shouted, pumping my fist in the air.

"It ain't gonna be no vacation for me. I have to go to summer school," my friend, Isaac, complained as we walked home from school.

"I still don't understand how you flunking classes in the 8th grade. I mean we don't even do shit," I said, shaking my head.

"Whatever, Xavier. Everybody can't be a fuckin' genius like you. You don't even have to open a book and already know all the answers. You've always been that way," Isaac huffed, shaking his head.

"You got excuses for everything." I shrugged, quickly losing interest in the conversation because my thirteen-year-old eyes were fixated on the lyrical battle taking place right in front of me. There was a small crowd surrounding the guys who looked to be only a few years older than me. As I walked closer, not only was I able to witness but I could hear them spitting lyrics back and forth to each other. It was a word battle that I had never seen before and the more the verbiage escalated the more intrigued I became.

"Xavier, come on! We need to get home," I heard Isaac call out, but I was paying him no mind. I wanted in on the battle. It was crazy. I had never rapped a lyric a day in my life, but hearing these two young guys who looked just like me, going at it had me mesmerized. Yeah, I had watched rappers on television and heard them on the radio, but being so up close and personal had this profound affect on me.

"Yo, Xavier we need to go!" Isaac yelled, grabbing my arm. "You know I'm on punishment. My moms told me I betta come straight home after school. So let's go or I'ma get in trouble," Isaac complained.

"Man, stop yo' whining. Besides, you on punishment... not me. Take yo' ass home. I'ma stay here and watch this rap battle," I said dropping my book bag. I was ready to make this corner block my home for the rest of the afternoon.

"Yo' you buggin'! I thought you were gon' come to my house and keep me company. My mom said you the only friend I can have over."

"Go 'head." I waved my hand, signaling Isaac to keep it moving. "I'll be over there in a minute."

Isaac glanced at me and then the two guys rapping. "Why you so interested in what they doing?" he questioned, not able to hide his confusion. It was written all over his face.

"'Cause they doing what I'ma do." I nodded my head with confidence.

"And what's that... run yo' mouth? You already know how to do that."

"Nah, dummy!" I shook my head. "I'ma be a rapper."

Isaac fell out laughing. He bent over, dropping his book bag, making this major production like he heard the funniest joke ever. "X, you got mad jokes. So you gon' be on the corner like these two clowns and call yo'self a rapper," he sneered. Isaac was now holding his stomach like he was laughing so hard that he had stomach cramps or something.

"Go 'head... keep laughing." I chuckled. "Wait and see. Not only am I gonna be a rapper. But the streets gon' say I was wanna the best that ever did it. I'ma be a star." Then I paused for a second before continuing. "Fuck a star. I'ma be a superstar." I smiled looking towards the clouds, seeing my vision up in the blue sky."

"Yo, you have officially lost yo' mind," Isaac snorted. "When you get yo' head up outta those clouds, stop by the crib. I'll be waiting on you so we can play some video games."

"Cool." I nodded as Isaac hurried off, but I never made it to his crib that day. I stayed on the block like my shoes were glued to the cement. That afternoon, on a sunny day in Queens, New York, I realized just how I would create my legacy. "Get ready world, 'cause I will be king," I mumbled under my breath as I continued to study the two young men who had become my inspiration.

Chapter Two

Practice Makes Perfect

Knock... knock... knock... knock... knock... knock

After the non-stop knocking I had no choice but to open the door. "Yes!" my one word dripped of irritation.

"Don't yes me!" my mom snapped, with her hand firmly pressed against her waist. "And turn down that music! It's so loud I can barely hear myself talk."

"I guess that's why you yelling," I said mockingly, before turning down the radio. I could feel my mother's eyes burning a hole in my back with her stare.

"Boy, you better watch that tone," she warned.

"I apologize." I made sure to sound sincere because I didn't want any drama with my mother. All I wanted was for her to get out my bedroom so I could get back to doing what was now my only passion.

"I wanted to let you know that dinner is ready."

"Thanks. I'll be down in a minute," I said, about to turn my music back up.

"No, you are going to come down now," she shot back, stressing the word now.

"Just give me a few more minutes," I countered, trying to contain my annoyance.

"Xavier, you've been locked away in this room all day. You need to come out and at least eat a hot meal. You can't stay in here doing nothing."

"That's what you call what I'm doing... nothing!" I popped. "This ain't nothing," I huffed, grabbing the stacks of papers on top of my bed, with the hundreds of lyrics I had written. "I'm practicing."

"Practicing what?" My mom's mouth frowned up. She had that same confused look on her face that Isaac had given me weeks ago.

"I finally figured out what I want to do with my life."

"Okay, and it includes you staying locked away in your room listening to loud music. What sorta life is that?"

"It's the life of a rapper."

"What in the world is a rapper? That doesn't sound like something that will be beneficial to your life."

"These are rappers." I turned up the volume on the radio and let the sounds of Erik B & Rakim blast through the speakers. I began bopping my head and spitting rhymes I made up off the top of my head to the beat. I found myself freestyling and to my surprise it actually sounded good. Maybe better than anything I had written down on all the paper scattered around my room.

"Boy, where you learn to say all that stuff?" My mom finally questioned after listening to me spit lyrics for a few minutes.

"I just made it up. It sounded nice… right?" I grinned, feeling pleased with myself.

"You made all that up, just now?" My mom asked with astonishment.

"I sure did."

"I guess you have been doing something

while locked up in this room," she beamed. My mom gave me that sweet smile she would get when she was proud of me. "Well I'll be. My son is going to be a rapper." She smiled before wrapping her arms around my chest giving me a warm hug.

My mother's reaction to my impromptu performance meant more to me than anything in the world. Her and my father were completely old school. The only music they listened to was by artists like Marvin Gaye, The Temptations, Otis Redding, people like that. When my mom wondered what a rapper was, she meant that shit. This was brand new to her, but yet she embraced it and I knew it was because she loved me and because she thought I was good at it. There was one thing I knew about my mother. If I had sucked or if she thought I would go out there and embarrass myself, she would be the first person to tell me that this ain't it for me. I always respected her honesty. My mother never wanted to hurt my feelings, but at the same time she didn't believe in telling me lies or selling me dreams. She was almost a truth teller to a fault.

But now that I had gotten my mom's stamp of approval and she said her son was going to be a rapper, it was a done deal. There was no denying my destiny. My mother's words had sealed my fate.

"Where you been hiding? I thought you had moved outta Queens, " Isaac joked when I walked up on him and some other neighborhood boys shooting hoops at the park. "It's the end of the summer... we 'bout to start back school. What made you decide to finally come out the house?"

"Man, be quiet and throw me the ball." I chuckled, happy to be amongst some of my friends. I had shut myself off from the world for the last couple months as I spent day and night honing my rap skills.

"Yo, Xavier has honored us with his presence. Let me find out we 'bout to get snow in the middle of summer," Dante, another one of my friends from school chimed in, taking the ball from Isaac and dunking it.

"I know you ain't tryna show off," I mocked, reaching for the loose ball, then doing a backwards spin before dunking the ball in Dante's face.

All you heard was jeers echoing on the court from the guys watching the slam dunk I just did on Dante.

"That was nice!" Isaac smirked, giving me some dap.

"What, you thought I had fell off my hoop game 'cause I ain't been out here," I stated to no one in particular.

Funny thing was, for years, I was known for being one of the best shooters in Queens. I had always been tall for my age, but also swift so playing basketball came naturally for me. There were already coaches from different schools coming to my parents trying to recruit me. A lot of people in the neighborhood assumed that I would pursue a career in basketball. I mean it was a dream for a lot of kids my age to one day play in the NBA, but it was a dream that most knew would never come true. But in my case it seemed to be a real possibility. There was only one problem... I had absolutely zero interest. Shooting hoops was like a past time hobby for me. It was fun every once in awhile, but my heart wasn't in it. I only felt passion and excitement for one thing and that was rapping.

"Man, we stomped ya," Isaac bragged as we started to leave the park after beating Dante and the team he put together for a bball game.

"I don't know what you bragging for. It was yo' man that got all the shots," one of Dante's boys said being playful but serious.

"Don't matter. I was on his team so that means I get the win too. Ain't that right, X?"

I heard the conversation, but I wasn't listening, if that makes any sense. The reason why was because we had come up on a heated rap battle and I wanted in.

"Them niggas nice," Dante said as we huddled around the two guys. We all instantly got caught up, mainly because it was difficult to decipher who was better. One would go in with a dope metaphor then the other would come right back with something equally hot.

I felt the blood flowing through my body rapidly heating up from my excitement of watching everything transpire in front of me. I kept leaning forward wanting to jump in between the guys and add my two cents, but I couldn't do it. For what felt like the very first time in my life, I was scared. Everything had always come so easy... sports, schoolwork, and even girls liking me. This sense of fear that I wasn't used to had me feeling uneasy and I didn't like that shit at all.

I watched as Isaac, Dante, and the rest of the fellas cheered the dudes on. Everyone was so hyped, including me but my fear was holding me back from doing what my heart wanted. My hands began to get sweaty. I was itching to see if I was truly built for this or would I only be a bedroom rapper. As everyone was enjoying the rap battle from an entertainment standpoint, I was battling with myself if I was gon' go hard or go the fuck home.

"Fuck it," I mumbled. I never wanted to be the type of person that let fear dictate my moves. I looked at this situation as a test and it was one I refused to fail.

"Xavier, what the fuck is you doing!" I heard Isaac yell out but it was too late. I had thrown my tall skinny ass dead in the middle of what I was now calling a cypher.

The two dudes paused for a minute looking at me and then at each other. Although they didn't say it with words, their facial expressions clearly was saying, what the fuck is he doing. I used the moment of silence in my favor. I took the opportunity to jump right in and start spitting. I decided to skip an introduction and go straight to using intricate and creative punchlines. I only had a very small window to make an impression so I needed to take advantage of every second.

Once I got started, the words began flowing effortlessly. Instead of standing in front of a crowd of a few, I imagined myself on a stage performing in front of thousands of fans. As my mind brought that vision to life, I went from creative punchlines to the next level of a hyper egotistical war of words and linguistic play.

"What ain't this nigga good at?" I heard one of Dante's friends gasp, holding his hand up as I ripped rhymes on some a cappella shit. Watching my lyrics and flow turn mug faces into stunned believers, gave me the boost I needed to make what started off as a rap battle between two dudes that were equally nice into me coming out the clear winner.

Don't get me wrong, neither one of those dudes willingly handed me over a win. The moment they realized I didn't come to play but to slay they stepped up their rhymes even more. They didn't hold anything back. Delivering bars after bars, but none of that mattered. For every slick line they tossed out, I threw some shit back even harder. This right here was what you called putting in work. The same way college students got internships to get hands-on experience in their designated field. This was how real rappers developed their craft. Because once you mastered how to battle rap, no one could break your confidence and that was the key competent to becoming a great rapper. Whether it was true or not, believing you are the best to ever do it, is what made you a beast.

That late summer afternoon in Queens, New York, I was no longer destined to remain a bedroom rapper. I had conquered my fear and I was ready to take the world by storm one rap battle at a time. I was now reaping the benefits of locking myself away in my bedroom all summer long. Practice did make perfect.

Chapter Three

Not My Time

It seems the older you get, the faster time goes by. Even though I was still a teenager, I was no longer a thirteen-year-old boy, I was now a sixteen-year-old young man. At least that's how I felt. Call it adolescent dreams, but I imagined my life to be a lot different than it was right now. As I sat in my math class halfway listening to the teacher, I contemplated what the fuck I was doing wrong. For the last three years I had participated in every corner rap battle I could. Did any and every local talent show and won them all, but nothing came out of it. In my mind, I figured somebody would've discovered me by now and put me on, but it never happened. For the first time, I was beginning to wonder if I would ever catch my big break.

When I heard the bell ring, signaling that class was over, I snapped out of my daydreaming. As I was headed out the door, I heard my teacher call out my name. I turned around slowly dreading to have a conversation with her. This was my last class and all I wanted to do was get the fuck outta here.

"Is there a problem, Mrs. Connors?"

"There's no problem, Xavier. I just wanted to speak to you about something."

"I'm sorta in a rush. I really need to get home."

"It will only take a few minutes. Please have a seat."

I reluctantly sat down at the desk in front of where Mrs. Connors was standing. "So what do you want to talk to me about?"

"Xavier, during class I don't seem to have your attention which concerns me."

"This must be about the test we had

yesterday. I've had a lot going on so I didn't have a chance to study. I'll do better next time and I promise to pay more attention in class. Now that we've cleared that up, can I go now?" I asked starting to stand up.

"See, Xavier, that's what has me concerned."

"What, I told you I'd do better next time. It's only one test."

"You actually got the highest grade in the class on that test."

"Then what's the problem?"

"I don't think you're being challenged enough in this class. You didn't study, but you got every math problem correct but one. You're an extremely bright young man, Xavier."

"Well thank you," I said. I wasn't sure what point my teacher was trying to make, but I wanted her to hurry up and get to it.

"There is a school in Manhattan for exceptionally bright students and I think you should apply."

"Mrs. Connors, thank you for thinking of me, but I'm sure a school like that is crazy expensive and my parents ain't got it like that."

"That doesn't matter, Xavier. If you were accepted, which I believe you would have an excellent chance, they would give you a full scholarship. You wouldn't have to pay for anything," she informed me. "Here," Mrs. Connors continued, handing me a packet. "This is information about the school. Read over it. Discuss it with your parents. But I believe this would be a wonderful opportunity for you. I'll be more than happy to help you with all the paperwork."

"Why are you doing this? I'm sure you have lots of students that are just as smart as me. Are you giving them packets too?"

"To answer your question honestly. No, I don't. In my twenty years of teaching high school students, you're the first one I've ever given this packet to. I've spoken to your other teachers and they all say the same thing. You're the brightest student in their class without even putting forth any effort. You have so much potential, Xavier. I simply want to lead you in the right direction."

"I appreciate your help, Mrs. Connor. I'll read over the info and let you know what I decide."

"Please do and make sure to share the information with your parents."

"I will," I lied, already halfway out the door. I didn't give a fuck about some fancy school. The conversation with my teacher only accomplished one thing... further pissing me off. Here was another so-called opportunity being given to me, but not the one I wanted. People were constantly trying to reward me for shit I put no effort into.

But the one thing I was busting my ass for on a daily basis, was getting me absolutely nowhere.

"Fuck this shit man!" I scoffed, kicking the exit door open on my way out the building.

"You haven't said a word since you sat down for dinner. Is everything okay?" my mom asked.

"Everything is fine," I replied barely touching my food.

"Your mother puts a lot of hard work into preparing these meals every night. The least you can do is eat your food."

"Relax, honey. It's fine," my mother said to my father trying to keep the peace.

"You don't like what your mother cooked?" my dad questioned in a belligerent tone, but I wouldn't take the bait.

"I'm not really hungry that's all." I had a lot on my mind but I kept my cool.

"You seem distracted, son. Would it have anything to do with that prep school in the city?"

My mother's question caught me off guard. "How do you know about that?"

"Earlier today I was putting some of your clothes away and saw the pamphlet on top of your dresser. I also saw the note your teacher had addressed to us," my mother explained.

"Your teacher sent a letter home and you never gave it to us?" my father wanted to know.

"Yes, but..."

"But nothing," my dad interjected. "Boy, you go get that letter right now."

"Mom just said she saw the letter so I'm sure she read it."

"I don't care what your mother read. I want to read the letter. Now go get it."

I excused myself from the table and headed to my bedroom to get the letter. I could hear my mother telling my dad to calm down, but he seemed determined to make shit difficult for me tonight.

"Here you go," I said handing my dad the letter. I sat back down and took a sip of juice. I tried to take a bite of the chicken on my plate, but by now I had completely lost my appetite. I peeped my dad reading over the letter Mrs. Connors had written. His entire face was buried in the paper like he didn't want to miss one word.

"When you gon' take this test so you can attend this school?" my dad wanted to know.

"I'm not sure."

"What do you mean you're not sure... what you waiting for?" he demanded.

"I haven't decided if I even want to go or not."

"Xavier, this is a wonderful opportunity. Why wouldn't you want to attend, baby?" my mom questioned with concern.

"I don't know. I just..."

"I just nothing!" my dad belted, slamming the palm of his hand on the dinner table. "This ain't even up for discussion. You will be taking that test and you better do good so you can get yo' ass in that school."

"Don't you think it should be my decision if I want to attend this school or not?"

"Of course..." my mother started.

"Of course my ass!" my dad blurted cutting her off. "It's about time you start figuring out what you gon' do with your life and a school like this will help you do that."

"I already know what I'm going to do with my life," I stated, still keeping my cool.

"And what's that?" My dad leaned back in his chair folding his arms.

"I've decided to pursue my rap career."

"Your rap career. Boy, if you don't get yo' head out of them damn clouds. We entertained that foolishness when you were thirteen and fourteen, but you sixteen now. You'll be a grown man, having to pay your own bills before you know it. It's time you start setting real goals for yourself instead of these make believe fantasies."

"This isn't a fantasy for me. Being a rapper is the only thing I want for my life."

"Oh please." My dad shook his head. "Hell, it was my dream to play in the NFL. But I knew that was never going to happen, so I set realistic goals for myself and it's about time you started doing the same."

"It's not my fault you gave up on your dream and settled on some mid-level position at a local bank."

"That mid-level position is what keeps a roof over your head and food on this table," my father stood up and yelled.

"Harold, please have a seat and calm down," she pleaded.

"You think these bills pay themselves. You wait until you have your own damn family to support and then you talk to me about what you will and won't settle for in life."

I had clearly hit a nerve with my father because I couldn't remember a time I had ever seen him look so angry. It wasn't my intention to rile him up, but I also needed him to understand that this rap shit wasn't just some school kid's hobby for me. This shit was real. It ran through my blood and I wasn't going to let nothing or no one stop me from making it happen.

"Listen, Dad. I'm sorry if you feel that I've disrespected you in any way. I appreciate everything you do for our family." I caught my mother smiling as the apologetic words were coming out my mouth. "I know that you work hard and you've always provided for us. All I want is a chance to one day be able to provide for my own family by doing what I love to do."

"Son, I wish I could tell you that life was that easy, but it's not. The likelihood of you having a career as a rapper is zero to none. You may not want to hear that, but as your father it's my obligation to tell you the truth."

"That may be your truth, but I respectively decline to make it mine. Now if you both will excuse me."

Before I even had a chance to make it to my bedroom and close the door, my mother was right on my back. I wasn't in the mood to continue the conversation, but I also didn't want to hurt her feelings by turning her away. When she looked in my eyes I couldn't deny her.

"Come on in," I said sitting down on my bed. She sat down right next to me and took my hand.

"My beautiful baby," she said rubbing the side of my cheek. "I know you think you're almost grown, but you're still my baby and always will be."

"Mom, why are your eyes watering up? Don't do that." I shook my head. My mother had this way of making me feel guilty for no reason and I hated that.

"One day when you have your own child you'll understand these tears in my eyes. It's called unconditional love. The type of love that only a parent and a child share."

"I don't know if Pops would agree with that," I mocked.

"Stop it. Your father loves you so much. It's just that sometimes he has a hard time understanding you. He sees life as black and white. He doesn't get that some people fall in the gray area... people like you."

"But you get it, huh?"

"Of course I do. You're my son. I knew you were different while I was carrying you in my stomach. You were always special and special people go about life different then us normal folks." She laughed.

"I wish Dad could understand and let me be." I pulled my hand away from my mom becoming frustrated replaying what my father had said to me.

"If your father let you be then that would mean he didn't care, but he does."

"I don't want to be stuck at some school,

learning things I could care less about. I want to be a rapper."

"And you will be, son."

"You don't believe that. You're just saying it to make me feel better."

"You know me better than that. I don't say nothing that I don't mean. From the day you stood in this very room in front of that radio and put on that spontaneous performance I knew you would be a rapper."

"You mean that... forreal?"

"There's not a doubt in my mind."

"Then why can't you tell Pops that?"

"I have, but your father is stubborn. But he'll believe it once he hears your first song on the radio. Or when we attend your first concert. All that will happen for you at the right time."

"But when is my time?"

"Only God knows that. You have to believe that He is the best of planners. While God is doing His part, you need to do yours."

"And what would that be?"

"While you're pursuing your dream of becoming a rapper superstar, you still gotta go to school."

"True."

"So why not at least go to the best school you can and get the best education possible."

"I guess that means you want me to apply to that prep school."

"Of course I do. Nothing in life is by accident. There is a reason this opportunity has been presented to you. All I ask is that you at least take the test and see how you do."

"Oh, I'll ace that test," I said without hesitation. "You don't have to worry about that."

"I still get a kick out of you." She giggled. "So do we have a deal? You'll attend that prep school and I'll work on getting your father to accept that being a rapper is your plan A. Everything else is simply a backup."

"We have a deal. All we have to do is shake on it." I extended my hand and my mother quickly latched on to it.

"I'm truly proud of you, Xavier. God couldn't have blessed me with a more special child. You are growing up to be such an exceptional young man. Hell, you're better than exceptional," she gushed.

"What's better than exceptional," I joked.

"Geesh, I don't know. You're the wordsmith. You tell me... maybe remarkable, extraordinary, or how about supreme." My mother nodded, winking her eye. "I like that. You're a supreme young man." She then kissed my forehead like she used to do when I was five or six years old.

"Supreme... yeah I do like that." I nodded, repeating the word over and over again. "I mean what tops being supreme. It gets no better than that."

"I couldn't agree with you more."

"Thanks mom." I smiled, now giving her a kiss of my own.

"Thanks for what?"

"For giving me my new rap name."

"Huh?! What are you talking about?" My mother gave me this look of bewilderment.

"From this day forward I'm going by a new name. It's time for the world to get introduced to Supreme."

Chapter Four

Supreme

From the time I left for school in the morning, until the final bell rang in the afternoon, I was known as Xavier Mills. But the moment I walked out those double doors and hit the street, I became Supreme. The rap name my mother unwittingly gave me. It was the perfect fit for my newfound confidence and determination.

Now that I was attending school in the city,

I found new spots to participate in rap battles. Being in a different environment also triggered another level of creativity with my music. I had no idea that my commute to the City on the subway every morning and night would expand my mind the way it did. I had grown up in the same neighborhood around the same people all my life. Now that I had been exposed to an entire new array of faces, I had even more stories to tell through my lyrics.

"I had a chance to see you going at it with that dude yesterday and you killed it. I had no idea you had skills like that."

I turned all the way around so I could see who was talking to me. I had like zero friends at my new school, which was by choice so I was completely baffled as to who was talking to me.

"I'm sorry but do I know you?" I frowned at the nerdy, unremarkable looking kid sitting behind me in the school library.

"I'm Bailey," he perked up and said, flicking his straggly blond hair from over his eye.

"Okay. I still don't know you."

"Oh I get that, but I know who you are. You're a rapper."

"And you know this how?"

"Like I was saying you were at that underground spot a lot of kids hang out at. Yesterday was the first time I saw you, but maybe because you were there for the rap battle they have every Wednesday."

"Yeah. Someone put me on to it so I decided to check it out."

"Whoever did I want to thank them because you are the best rapper I've ever seen come in there. You destroyed that dude man!" he exclaimed sounding extra geeky.

"Thanks," I replied unimpressed. "He wasn't much competition."

"Maybe not for you, but that's just how great you are." Bailey chuckled, in almost like a pig snorting sound. He was a geek foreal I thought.

"Appreciate it."

As the boy continued rambling I had turned back around in my chair to hit the books. At this new school they gave students a lot of freedom in terms of their preferred learning style and studying, but you were hit with a test almost every other day. On top of that we were basically taking college courses. So although it was still easy for me to learn the material, the fast pace at which it was given to us, required me to set time aside for my academics. I wasn't used to that. I wanted to invest all my time on my rhymes. But I made a promise to my mother to graduate with honors and I planned to keep it.

"Nah, man, I appreciate you. You're amazing and..." At this point I was trying to block dude out. I was over his nonstop showering of praises. I was one second from telling his annoying ass to shut the fuck up until he said something that sparked my interest.

"I was so stoked that I told my brother who works at Def Jam that he has to hear you rhyme because..."

"Your brother works at Def Jam?" I didn't even let Bailey finish what he was saying. All I heard was Def Jam.

"Yeah... yeah."

"Def Jam. The label that has LL Cool J, EPMD, and Public Enemy... that Def Jam?" I caught my mouth about to drop from amazement so I quickly pulled myself together.

"Yeah! Yeah! That Def Jam." Bailey's beady green eyes had widened. He seemed more excited then me. "I begged him to come listen to you, but he laughed at me. He said there was no way I went to school with anybody that could rap anything other than a nursery rhyme." Then Bailey hit me with the pig snort chuckle my ears refused to get used to.

"How did your brother get a job at Def Jam?" I was staring at Bailey's goofy ass and I couldn't wrap my mind around how he had a brother working at the hottest hip hop label in the country.

"Oh, well you see my dad is a partner at the law firm that represents Def Jam. They're one of their clients. I guess it was a favor you know because my brother has like a really high ranking position over there too."

"Got you. That makes sense," I said clutching my fingers through each other. My mind was spinning. Bailey's brother might be the plug I needed to catch my big break and I had to figure out how to meet him.

"There's this place in Harlem that has rap battles too. I've never been because I heard it's a little... you know... kinda tough... aha ha—" Before Bailey was able to do his typical pig snort chuckle I stopped him.

"I get what you mean," I said putting my hand up gesturing for him to stop.

"I heard a lot of really cool people come through there. I really want to go you know... but ummm maybe if you went I could," Bailey sounded nervous not finishing his sentence, but I knew what he wanted to say.

"You think it would be worth me making an appearance there?"

"For sure! Can I come with you?" he blurted out jumping out his chair. Other students in the library looked up startled by Bailey's sudden outburst.

"Have a seat, Bailey," I said motioning my hand for him to sit down.

"Sorry about that. I'm a little excited. I've heard so much about that place. My brother and a guy he works with mentioned discovering a new artist there."

"Really... do you think you can get your brother to come see me battle there?"

"For sure! That would be incredible! How about this Friday?"

"Let's do it. Make sure you confirm everything with your brother."

"I will. This will score me major cool points with my brother. By the way, I know you're school name is Xavier, but what's your like stage name? It was so loud in that place I didn't catch it."

"Supreme. I go by Supreme."

"It seems like it's been forever since we hung out," Isaac said as we caught the train in Queens to meet Bailey in the city.

"Yeah, I know. Between my commute to and from school I barely have time to do shit."

"How you digging that school? I heard it's some real high posh shit."

"It's straight. A lot of rich kids do go there, but they're pretty chill. Everybody just tryna win. It's mad competitive with the academics, but other than that it's cool." I shrugged.

"I bet, but you probably smarter then all those rich kids. Have to be to get in a school like that with a full scholarship." Isaac laughed, playfully shoving me on the arm.

"It ain't as easy as I thought it would be, but I'm maintaining. Just ready to graduate so I can focus on my music full time, but that's a long way off."

"I swear when you first mentioned this rap shit a long time ago I thought it was just a phase you going through. But now here we are on our way to Harlem for you to participate in a rap battle. Thanks for letting me tag along."

"Glad you were able to come. I'm sure Bailey gon' be happy too. He don't wanna be standing solo with nobody to talk to while I'm on stage."

"What he shy or something?"

"Nah, he a cool lil' white boy. But this ain't really his scene although he would like it to be." I laughed. "His brother is coming though, but he's gonna meet us there so he'll appreciate yo' company."

"Whatever to all that, I can't wait to see you in action. Don't let me down. You betta represent for Queens up there."

"I will. I'ma kill it. I'ma go at it like my life depends on it. I put that on everything." I was serious too because I did feel like in a lot of ways my life depended on it. I told Isaac that Bailey's brother was coming, but I left out the fact he worked for Def Jam. Tonight I was rapping like this was my one shot to score a record deal. No other opportunities were coming my way so I felt it was now or never.

By the time we met up with Bailey and made it to Harlem the show was about to start. There were cars lined up the street and a bunch of people still waiting to get inside.

"I can't believe how crowded it is," I commented when we made our way to a side entrance where the people that were participating in the battle were supposed to check in at.

"I told you this was the place to be," Bailey gushed with enthusiasm.

"Did you see your brother out there on the way in?" I questioned.

"No I didn't, but he'll be here," Bailey said as we made our way through the door.

As soon as we stepped inside, the security at the front door led us down some narrow stairs.

It was dark and reeked of cigarette smoke and weed. The stairs then transitioned into what felt like a confined tunnel. The space was so small I figured the stage would be the size of a closet.

"What kinda rap battles they got poppin' off in this hole in the wall," Isaac mumbled under his breath.

"I'm wondering the same thing," I said on the low. "I know this the right spot but damn."

"This way!" All three of us jumped simultaneously when out of nowhere we heard a loud boisterous voice yell out from the distance. It was so dark we couldn't even place a face with the voice. When we got to the end of the hall there was a large steel door. We stood there and I figured we were all pondering the same thing... what's behind this big ass door.

"I guess I better open it." When I reached over to put my hand on the knob, the door flung open on some magic shit.

"This place is so cool even cooler then I thought it would be," Bailey beamed, swiftly stepping between Isaac and me so he was the first person through the door.

"What's up wit' yo' friend?" Isaac asked glancing over in my direction.

"Dude goofy. Don't pay him no mind," I said brushing off Isaac's comment. I needed to focus on this battle. I couldn't afford to get distracted by Bailey's odd ass.

"Oh shit, check this place out," I heard Isaac say as entered right after Bailey. I couldn't see anything yet because there were a few people blocking my view, but once I got inside I understood what Isaac meant.

"Who would've ever thought all this was hidden behind that door," I said truly amazed. That narrow path led to a gigantic open space that could fit hundreds if not a couple thousand of people. It was already filled close to capacity. Unlike the dirty hallway we traveled to get here, the actual space was clean and odor free.

"Which one of you is the artist?" a short stocky man with an even heavier New York accent then my father asked.

"That would be my main man, Supreme," Bailey spoke up and said. He then ran back towards me and patted me on the shoulders.

"Cool. If you all are just his friends then you need to get off this stage and join the crowd. Only management is allowed on the stage," the stocky man informed us.

"Oh we are his manager. I'm Bailey and that's Isaac." I eyed Bailey who was grinning like a champ. I didn't want either one of them to get stuck in that massive crowd so I played along.

"Yeah, they my managers." I nodded. The man glanced over at Isaac and then back at Bailey and me like he wasn't completely sold on what we said, but he let it slide.

"A'ight. You'll hear your name called when we're ready for you, so stay right here until then. We don't want any of the artists talking to each other until it's your time to step up. Understood?"

"Understood," I replied.

"I'm glad you said that shit 'cause I damn sure didn't feel like standing over there with all them people," Isaac said with a sigh of relief once the man had walked away.

"Yeah, I'm just ready for the show to start," I huffed.

"Feeling anxious?" Bailey smirked.

"Nah, just ready to win."

"You feeling mighty confident over there," Isaac joked.

"Ain't no other way to be. I'm sure every motherfucker on this stage is feeling confident. If not they in the wrong spot. This rap battle shit ain't for a weak, scared nigga," I made clear.

"I feel you. Hope you can deliver the goods 'cause they're a lot of heads up in this joint. I would hate for you to get booed off the stage." Isaac laughed.

"Me too!" I said joining in on Isaac's laughing.

"'Cause it's damn sure a packed house," I added, staring out into the crowd. "Do you see your brother out there?" I asked Bailey while the lights were still on.

"I do think I see him over there in the back corner," Bailey said pointing out into the crowd. "I'm sure he's here, but don't worry about that right now. You need to focus on your performance."

Right after Bailey said that the lights went out and the place went dim. Then some smoke type shit surrounded the stage with a limelight shining in the center. I figured that was the spot we would stand. All of a sudden my heart rate sped up. I hadn't felt this sort of adrenalin rush since the time I ambushed the rap battle taking place in the park when I was thirteen. I wasn't sure if this feeling was good or bad. Then the palm of my hands began to get sweaty.

"You alright, X?" I heard Isaac ask me.

"Yeah, why you ask me that?"

"'Cause you sweatin'" he replied, nodding his head towards my forehead.

"I'm good, just a little hot," I said, taking the back of my hand and wiping away the sweat.

"Damn, it's a little cold to me," Isaac said zipping up his jacket. He was right. They had the AC blasting, but I didn't want to admit I was sweating due to nervousness.

Supreme get yo' mind right. This ain't the time to be scared. You got way too much on the line. Bailey's brother probably watching you right now. If you want this label deal you better straighten the fuck up, I thought trying to hype myself up.

"Man, you don't hear them calling you! It's your turn. You betta get up there!" I heard Isaac say to me snapping me out of my get-yourself-pumped speech.

"Yeah, go ahead," Bailey chimed in pushing me forward.

I felt like I was walking in slow motion. I couldn't even see what was ahead of me. It seemed pitch black because I was blinded by the bright lights. With each step I wondered if I was going to make a wrong move and fall off the stage. But then once I took my spot, making my entrance in the center of the stage, I could now see the faces in the crowd and I heard the beat drop. It was like a switch went off. Everything clicked. The fear that was engulfing me mere seconds ago dispersed just as quickly.

This is my crowd. They are here for me and I'm about to deliver, I said to myself and just like that I went from being Xavier Mills to Supreme.

Chapter Five

Come Up

"Yo you murdered that shit!! I can't believe I know you," Isaac said giving me a pound. "Proud of you, man. I remember you being nice, but when did you get so ill?" he continued shaking his head as if in disbelief.

"I can't believe you won!" Bailey chimed in and yelled jumping up and down.

"Yo calm the fuck down," I said trying to keep

my voice down as all eyes were on us.

"Sorry about that." Bailey chuckled with his pig snort. "I'm just so happy for you," he said giving me a hug.

"Move back." I shrugged my shoulders and frowned pushing Bailey off of me without causing a scene. I did appreciate that he was genuinely happy for me, but Bailey had to learn to keep all that touchy feely shit in check. "Where your brother at? It's time we were introduced," I said wanting to get back to what was most important to me.

"Ummm he's...." Before Bailey could answer me, the stocky man interrupted us.

"Good job," he said handing me some money. "We'll see you here next week at the same time." He nodded his head and walked away. I looked down at the cash in my hand in shock. I had no idea I would win money if I won tonight.

"You got paid for this shit! No wonder you was out there rapping yo' ass off," Isaac popped.

"Yo, I had no idea there was money on the table. I was out there rapping for a deal."

"A deal?" Isaac questioned as if confused by what I said.

"Yeah, a record deal. Bailey's brother works at Def Jam. He came here tonight to see me battle so I had to put on," I finally revealed to Isaac.

"Word! Oh shit!" Isaac put his hand over the big ass smile on his face.

"I know right. It's about to be on. Come on, Bailey, let's go find your brother," I said turning my attention to him. I started walking forward, but noticed that Bailey was still behind me frozen in the same location. "What you waiting on?"

"Well... ummm..."

"Well ummm what?" I was pressed for an answer, but Bailey continued to stand there mum. For a minute I thought he was about to start twiddling his thumbs or some dumb shit.

"Clay isn't here."

"What he left? Why did you let your brother leave without introducing me to him?" I wanted to know.

Bailey's beady eyes darted around in every direction but mine before he finally said, "The thing is Clay was never here."

"Come again?" I stepped closer as if I wasn't hearing Bailey correctly. "Did you say your brother was never here? Nah, I must've heard you wrong 'cause before the show started you said he was standing over there," I said pointing in the direction Bailey showed me earlier.

"I remember that. You was pointing extra hard too," Isaac added which only made me more irritated with Bailey.

"I know. You seemed a little on edge and I didn't want to make it worse by telling you Clay wasn't coming. I wanted you to focus on winning and it worked... you won!"

"You fuckin' dumbass!" I barked, charging towards Bailey about to choke him up by his scrawny neck, but Isaac stopped me.

"Chill man. This ain't the place for that." Isaac stood in front of Bailey blocking my path.

"Supreme, I know you're upset, but I can explain. My brother had every intention of coming, but at the last minute the label sent him on the road with one of their artists. I only found out yesterday," Bailey explained.

"Why the fuck didn't you tell me that shit then? I'm searching for a motherfucker that ain't even here. You got me looking stupid. Running 'round here telling me a bold faced lie."

"It wasn't like that, Supreme, I swear. I'm your biggest fan. All I wanted you to do was come here and win. I didn't want the fact that my brother wasn't able to come to stop that from happening." Bailey stared down at the floor and for a second I thought the dude was about to cry. He appeared sincerely hurt that things didn't go down the way he told me they would. "I didn't mean to let you down."

"Don't worry about it. I can't believe I wasted

my motherfuckin' time. Guess this shit ain't meant to be," I scoffed.

"X, I know it ain't a record deal, but you did win tonight. You solidified yourself as a real contender in the game and on top of that you got paid for the shit. This won't no waste of time," Isaac said not making me feel no better.

"Fuck that! I didn't come to win a rap battle. I came to win a record deal."

"And that can still happen. I promise I'll make this up to you, Supreme. When my brother gets back in town you will meet him. I want him to see for himself how great you are."

"When will that be? When is your brother coming back?"

"I'm not exactly sure about that," Bailey admitted reluctantly. "But he will be back," he hastily added, visibly not wanting me to lose hope.

"Excuse me, youngin'. Can I speak to you for a sec." I turned my head in the direction I heard the deep bass voice coming from. My eyes landed on an average height dude with a curly hair box cut and slim build who looked to be in his early twenties. What caught my attention was the fresh gear he was wearing and the flashy jewelry.

"What's up?" My cool demeanor hid how impressed I was with his entire attire. Although

I couldn't afford it, I always respected a nigga whose exterior was on point. Even though his jewelry was flashy he kept his overall appearance low key, fly not gaudy.

"You did yo' thing out here tonight. I wanted to congratulate you," he said reaching out his hand for me to shake it, which I did. "I'm Rob."

"Supreme and thanks."

"I'm impressed wit' yo' flow. You got representation?"

"What you mean?"

"Like a manager.

"Nah... I mean some things are still being ironed out on that," I corrected myself thinking about Bailey and Isaac. I knew they weren't my managers, but since that's what we told the stocky man who worked here, I thought it best to keep the lie going for now.

"Oh okay, 'cause as ill as you are you most def need somebody to represent your interest."

"For sure," I agreed, beginning to wonder if that missing link was the reason shit wasn't falling into place the way I thought it should.

"Where you from?" he asked.

"Queens," I proudly responded representing for my borough.

"That's what's up. I be doing a lot of business in Queens." I was about to ask what sort of business, but I already had a pretty good idea. "Listen I ain't gon' hold you up. Like I said, wanted to let you know I was very impressed with the show you put on and I ain't easily impressed... trust me," he added.

"Thanks again. Appreciate the love."

"Take my number. If things don't work out with your current management I might be able to help you out. I have a lot of connections," he assured me.

"That nigga look like he got bank," Isaac commented as we watched him leave out with a couple of other guys that had that money swag too.

"That he does."

"What did he want with you?" Isaac inquired.

"To congratulate me and find out if I have a manager."

"What, he trying to manage you?"

"Maybe, I guess. He gave me his number; said he has a lot of connections."

"Are you gonna call him?"

"Not sure."

"What's the hesitation?"

"It's not hesitation; just making some observations. When and if I decide to get management it will be under my terms."

To my dismay, I was realizing the overnight

success I had envisioned was more like a winding road full of struggles and disappointments. If it had to be this difficult, it made no sense to me throwing in additional stress and potential complications by becoming aligned with the wrong manager. After the way things went down tonight, I did need to reconsider my game plan. If I had even a smidgen of a chance to open up some doors for myself, my next moves would have to be well calculated.

I was lying in my bed staring up at the ceiling with my eyes closed. I had the music turned up as loud as my ears would allow. My parents let me turn the basement into my bedroom a few months ago so I now had what I thought of as my own private musical heaven. I was letting the heavy, hard beats pump through my body before heading up the block to do some freestyle rapping with a couple of guys I was cool with. Once word got around the neighborhood that for the last several weeks I was the undisputed rap champ at that club in Harlem, people looked forward to hearing me spit. It had now become a Saturday ritual for me to hit the stoop with some of my boys and put on what would turn into a local show.

Finding different outlets to entertain people kept me from stressing over the fact that I wasn't making the sort of progress I wanted with my rap career. I was bummed over the fact that I still hadn't met Bailey's brother, but it wasn't his fault. To prove he wasn't full of shit, Bailey let me speak to Clay on the phone. It was only briefly, but he did confirm he was on the road with an artist. He wasn't sure when he would be back in town, but promised to meet with me once he was. I wanted to be like fuck that. I was ready to drop them bars for him over the phone, but he wasn't having it. He seemed preoccupied while I was speaking to him. I'm sure being on the road with an artist can do that to you, but I was wishing it were me that was on that road touring. Not only that, I didn't think Clay was convinced I was the real deal. He probably wanted to meet me in person to make sure his brother wasn't pulling a stunt on him. I couldn't blame him. If I had a brother like Bailey I would need firm confirmation too.

"Where you off to this afternoon?" my mother asked when I went upstairs to the kitchen to get me something to drink before heading out.

"You ask me the same question every Saturday and I always give you the same answer.

Nothing has changed." I laughed, opening the refrigerator.

"I guess I be checking to see if you're still committed or if you've given up."

"I ain't neva not never but neva, giving up."

My mom giggled at what I said and then smiled before saying, "That's all I wanted to hear. Go out there and have a good time and enjoy this weather. No need for that big coat you have on. It's pretty warm outside, especially for it to only be the end of March."

"Word. Maybe that's a sign that something good is going to happen for me today," I said with a slight grin. I then gave my mom a hug, hung my coat on the back of the chair in the kitchen, and headed out the door.

When I stepped outside, a nice breeze hit me in the face as the sun beamed down on me. My mom hadn't exaggerated. The weather was incredible. Being in the freezing cold all the time can put you in a bad mood sometime. So when you get an unexpected dose of warm weather it gives you a much needed boost. As I got closer to the spot, there was already a small crowd waiting. Everybody was in a good mood, making jokes, and laughing. That's what some sun and a nice breeze will do for a nigga.

"What up, Supreme!" Leon called out when

he noticed me walking up. That's when Isaac and some of my other boys joined in. I spoke to everybody; we made a few basic jokes and chilled on the stoop for a few.

"Yo, this weather is everything today. Why can't it stay like this. I'm over cold weather," Isaac complained.

"You and me both. People just be happier when the weather is nice," I said looking around, observing the nice vibe in the air.

"Not only that, the more them degrees go up the less clothes them chicks put on. I ain't seen this much skin since last summer," Isaac confessed.

"Then nigga that must mean you ain't fuckin' 'cause I was all up in some skins last night," Leon boasted. We all burst out laughing at what Leon said, everybody except for Isaac.

"Fuck you, Leon! I ain't trippin' over no pussy," Isaac scoffed.

"So says all niggas that ain't gettin' none," Leon countered. "Ain't that right, Supreme? I know these broads be throwing pussy yo' way. Girls were checkin' for you back when we was in middle school. I know they coming hard now that you got a lil' name wit' this rap shit."

All eyes shifted to me, waiting for my response. "Nah man, don't bring me into that petty shit. I ain't 'bout to have a pussy conversation wit' a bunch of niggas. Now, who ready to flow?" I said directing the conversation back to something I was interested in discussing because pussy wasn't it. For all I cared, them niggas could think I was a virgin, although I wasn't. But the only thing that gave me a continuous hard on was my music. Yeah, I had dealings with some chicks, but nothing serious and definitely not anything worth discussing. Between hitting the books and focusing on making it as a rapper, I barely had time or the energy to think about sex. On the rare occasion the urge did hit me for some female company, I would go see this girl Melanie that lived around the corner from me. She was low-key and that was the main reason she was the only chick I continued to deal with. I was a discreet type of dude so that made Melanie an ideal fit.

"Yeah, let's do this... I'm ready," my boy Tyreek said. He was always quick to get things jumpin'. Tyreek was nice with his too. His flow would start off slow and then he would start getting extra animated like a Busta Rhymes and get the crowd hyped up. Once that happened, we would all join in taking turns. I would always go last because by this point everyone was primarily showing up to see me.

The crowd had been growing with each week, but today it seemed to have quadrupled. I figured it was partially due to the weather. When it got hot folks would come out in droves. It was more females in the mix too and as I looked out at the pack of people I had to agree with Isaac. Most of these chicks were damn near naked. Some of them were even screaming out my name and reaching out their hands like they expected me to grab it. Even with all the flesh in my face I kept my focus. I didn't stop rhyming until I had the entire crowd, the men and the women in a frenzy.

"Supreme! Yo Supreme, let me to speak to you!" I heard someone yell out. I couldn't see a face amongst the swarm of people. Then the crowd divided in two making room for whoever was coming through.

"Damn, motherfuckers moving out the way like they scared or some shit," Isaac joked. We both zoomed in trying to see who was so important that everybody was stepping to the side with rapid speed. "Do you know him?" Isaac asked.

"I don't think so, but something about him do look kinda familiar," I said trying to place his face.

"My man, Supreme," the guy said taking my hand. "I see you still out here killin' it." Right when I was about to say who the fuck is you, the diamond emblem he was wearing around his neck awakened my memory. I noticed there was another dude standing slightly behind him, but he wasn't saying anything.

"Rob, I wasn't expecting to see you. How you been?"

"Good, but clearly not as good as you. The streets is loving you."

"Thanks man. So what brings you out here 'cause I know you ain't come to see me."

"I told you I handle a lot of business in Queens, but I came to handle some different business today. I wanted to introduce you to my man Arnez." Arnez stepped forward and shook my hand. He was wearing way less bling then Rob, but his watch looked like it cost more than all of Rob's jewelry combined.

"Rob has spoken very highly of you. I thought he was full of shit until I came out here and saw you for myself. They showing you a lot of love out here. That ain't an easy feat especially in Queens."

"You ain't gonna get no argument from me about that. For a minute I was contemplating whether they would be willing to show love for more than just one rapper from Queens. Since J-Rock has it on lock, I thought the odds were against me."

"Yeah, J-Rock out here doing it big in the rap game, but I can see why Queens is fuckin' wit' you. You got some serious talent, kid," Arnez said to me.

"I told you." Rob smiled nodding his head in agreement with Arnez. "How's that representation coming along?"

"It's coming. I'm taking my time. Making sure I don't make the wrong decision," I said, halfway telling the truth. I currently didn't have any options when it came to representation, but it was true I wanted to take my time and not make the wrong decision.

"That's smart," Arnez said. "You sign the wrong papers with the wrong people your career can end before it even has a chance to start."

"Exactly." I was glad this Arnez dude was seeing things my way.

"You have a lot of potential. You want to make sure whoever you team up with can give you what you need to make it. Rap is big business now. People are making a lot of money and as the artist you want to make sure you get your cut."

"No doubt."

"But while you're weighing your options, you should let me help you out. I think I can be very beneficial to your career... you know, help you jumpstart it. What do you think?" Arnez questioned.

I took my time responding to what Arnez said. I knew I was dealing with a man who was far from a dummy. He had probably been analyzing my every move before we was even introduced.

"Supreme, don't sleep on my man Arnez. I felt some kinda way when you never called me, but I understand you probably got a lot of people pulling at you right now so I'll let that go. But I believe in your talent that's why I brought Arnez here. If this man offers you help you don't decline," Rob stated. I sorta got a feeling that there was an underlying threat in Rob's last statement, but then again I could've been dissecting his words too much.

As if reading my mind, Arnez spoke up to ease my paranoia. "Listen, Supreme, I don't want you thinking about this too much. I believe you're a talented young man and I just want to help you accomplish your dreams. Luckily, I have a lot of extra money lying around." Arnez chuckled before continuing, "And I think investing in your career would be money well spent."

"I appreciate you believing in me, but like I said, I'm weighing my options when it comes to getting a manager."

"I get that and you don't have to sign any paperwork with me. I just wanna help. If you're happy with what I can do for you, then we can discuss a management deal. I think that sounds fair."

I was old enough and even wise enough at the age of seventeen, to know that help didn't come without strings attached when dealing with a man like Arnez. If he offered you his assistance, he had to believe there was something beneficial in it for him. There was danger lurking beneath his eyes, but I was hungry. I was hungry to get an edge on any potential competitors, which required something I didn't have… money and I was positive Arnez had plenty of that.

"I think that sounds fair too."

"Does that mean you're accepting my man's offer?" Rob wanted to confirm.

"Of course that's what Supreme means. I already told you this young man was smart," Arnez said with this devilish spark in his eyes.

"Yes, I'll accept your help. I'm looking forward to seeing what you can do."

"The first thing I'm gonna do is get you some new clothes," Arenz said eyeing my jeans, sweatshirt, and Timbs. "If you gon' be a rap star then you gotta look the part."

I was cool with my gear, but Arnez did have a point. I was in it to win and so I did need to look the part of a winner. I wanted to be able to walk into any room and to already look like I had signed that million dollar deal with a major label. It made me wonder if I looked the part would it finally make the part mine.

"I suppose some new clothes would be nice," I agreed.

"Good. My Saturday afternoon is open how about yours?" Arnez asked.

"You saying you wanna go now?" I questioned with a raised eyebrow.

"Yes, unless you got other things to do."

"Nah, I'm free. Let me tell my boys I'll get up with them later and we can go."

I could feel them watching me as I headed over to my friends. It was an uncomfortable feeling as if they were plotting on me. The problem was I wasn't sure if they were plotting my rise or my fall.

"You was over there talkin' to them niggas long enough," Isaac popped when I walked up.

"I was discussing some business with them."

"Business? From what I hear them niggas only handle one type of business. Ain't that right, Tyreek?" Isaac glanced over at Tyreek who was in the middle of telling Leon and some other guys a story, so he wasn't paying attention to what Isaac said.

"Isaac, I got this. The only business I'm discussing is about my music. Whatever else them dudes involved in has nothing to do with me," I wanted to make clear to Isaac.

"Keep telling yourself that. Dudes like that don't know how to separate the two so you better be careful," Isaac warned.

"I will be. I'll hit you up when I get back." I told all of them peace out before giving Isaac a chance to talk more shit. I knew he meant well and I wasn't jumping in with my eyes closed. I needed a come up and my gut instinct told me that with Arnez's help, he could be instrumental in making that happen.

Chapter Six

You Ready For This

I stood in the mirror admiring my appearance. I had the music blasting and I was rapping along to the beat. "Nigga, you is looking coffin sharp," I said grinning at my reflection. I couldn't even front, these new clothes had me feeling different; more confident. I know they say that clothes don't make a man, but yo, they sure give you that extra swag in your step. I grabbed my headphones and headed to the train so I could meet up with Bailey and his brother Clay in the city.

It had been weeks and I was beginning to think meeting with Clay would never happen. Then yesterday I got a call from Bailey. I figured it was about the upcoming test or something else school related, but instead he wanted to inform me his brother was back and ready to meet. While listening to music on the train ride to the city I was trying to decide which lyrics I would drop for Clay. I wanted to deliver something fresh unlike anything else out there right now. I struggled figuring out what that should be. By the time the train ride was over, I had walked a few blocks and now standing in front of Bailey's front door, I was still trying to make up my mind.

"Fuck it," I mumbled taking a deep breath before ringing the doorbell.

"Can I help you?" an older Hispanic woman who spoke with broken English, opened the door and asked. She was wearing a maid's uniform so I assumed she worked for them.

"Yes, I'm here..." Before I could continue Bailey appeared.

"Xavier, so glad you made it!" He came running up acting even more excited than usual. "Excuse me, Selita. I can take it from here." The

Hispanic lady gave me what seemed to be a suspicious look, staring me up and down then walked away. "Come on in," Bailey beamed, closing the door behind me.

"Wow, nice place," I said, glancing around the five story mansion. I don't know why I was surprised since Bailey's crib was located on one of the Upper East Side's finest townhouse blocks. The arched main entrance, the majestic living and dining rooms with towering ceilings and triple window openings had me dizzy.

"Come on, Clay and another guy he works with at Def Jam are out back," Bailey said, leading the way. All I could think was that one day I would be able to afford a place like this. I know most people would think that sounded crazy coming from a kid who lived in Queens, but I wasn't most people.

Bailey led me through French doors that opened up to a massive outdoor space with a garden and two terraces. The remarkable beauty of this place was unmatched by anything I had ever seen. My eyes had been open to a lifestyle I never knew existed. But once you're exposed to a world like this, there's no turning back. You can't even imagine ever living a simple life again.

"You must be Supreme," I heard someone say, interrupting my daydreaming.

"Yep, and you must be Clay."

"Yes, I am and this is my coworker, Desmond. He handles A&R."

"Nice to meet you," I said shaking Clay's and Desmond's hands.

Clay and Bailey definitely resembled. They both had those green beady eyes. But Clay dressed and had a much hipper look about himself. That probably came from being surrounded by hip hop and rappers on a daily basis. I also peeped a bit of shrewdness in his eyes. A trait I've never seen in his brother, Bailey. Desmond was a tall, slim black dude with dreads. He seemed mellow, like he just got done smoking a fat blunt.

"My brother has been going on an on about how great you are." I saw Bailey in the corner, eagerly nodding his head. "You certainly look the part," Clay commented, checking out the new all white sweat suit I had on. I even had a diamond stud that I had been trying my hardest to hide from my parents. But when Arnez offered to get it for me, I couldn't resist.

"Now we need to see if your flow measures up to your look," Desmond chimed in. His voice matched the mellow gaze he had in his eyes.

"No need wasting your time," I countered and just began flowing. I started off freestyling about everything from this big ass crib, to their clothes, to how they look then hit them with my regular shit and kept flipping it. It was obvious from the shocked looks on their faces they wasn't expecting none of that and that's the main reason why I did it. If we had kept going with the small talk I knew I would've been thinking too hard on what to say and possibly fucked shit up. So I dived in the deep end with no life jacket and went for it.

"Yo, we need to sign you right now!" Desmond stood up and said without hesitation.

"Hold up, Desmond." Clay motioned for Desmond to fall back as he tried to play it cool.

"Hold up, nothing! Ain't no sense in acting like this kid ain't the truth," Desmond popped back.

I understood what Clay was trying to do, but I respected the fact that Desmond wasn't about the mind games. I wasn't sure if it was because of the new gear I was rockin' or if all these years of being willing to rap for any and everybody had boosted my self-esteem up to some other level. But If Clay wanted to play mind games I was down for it.

"Surprisingly, my brother was right about you. You are the real deal, Supreme," Clay seemed reluctant to admit. "I think the label might be interested in signing you, but there's protocol we have to follow."

I caught Desmond rolling his eyes as if saying, this nigga here. "Do you think on Monday you can meet with some of our executives over at Def Jam? They're the ones who will make the final decision," Clay stated.

"I can stop by Monday after school," I said casually.

Clay gave me a I-can't-believe-he-just-said-that smile before he continued talking, "I'm sure you can miss one day of school."

"I really can't. I have a test on Monday."

"Yeah, he does. We're in the same class," Bailey's goofy ass said co-signing for me. I was starting to like Bailey more and more I thought, laughing to myself.

"Fine. We would hate for you to miss your test," Clay said sarcastically. "We can expect you after school gets out then."

"Yes, I'll be there but ummm, I need to be heading out."

"You have to leave so soon? I thought we could hang out for the rest of the day," Bailey said sounding disappointed.

"I would, but I have a studio session that I'm already running late for."

"Oh cool! Can I come? Please!" Bailey pleaded.

"Today's gonna be mad hectic but next time, man. I promise."

"So you have a studio session today?" Clay questioned, doing his best to sound like he didn't care, but I could tell he did.

"Yeah, I'm looking forward to it. I've been working on some new songs that I'm anxious to lay down on tracks."

"I see," Clay said, briefly locking eyes with Desmond. "Are you paying for the studio time out of pocket?"

"Hell no! I ain't got no money for that."

"So how are you paying for it, if you don't mind me asking. Studio time isn't cheap."

I purposely delayed answering Clay's question. I wanted him to drive himself a little crazy trying to come up with the answer to his own question. He started scratching the back of his head as if irritated by my silence.

"I don't wanna go into details 'cause it's not good business to discuss things that haven't been signed off on yet. I have a few other people that are interested in signing me. They asked if I would spit on one of their producer's tracks."

"I see. You know Def Jam is one of the hottest, if not the hottest, rap label. Every rapper wants to sign with us," Clay bragged.

"I can believe that."

"Good. Then I'm sure that means you won't be making any decisions about who you'll sign with until you see our offer."

"This is the first I'm hearing about an offer. I thought you said I had to meet with the executives over at Def Jam before that decision was made."

"That's only a formality." Clay then paused and turned his attention to Desmond. "I think we're in agreement that Supreme should be signed to the label."

"Like I stated from the jump, the kid is a winner. You damn right we need to sign him. I don't know what more needs to be said." Desmond shrugged.

"I agree. So there you have it, Supreme. We want you on Def Jam."

"That's what's up, Clay. I look forward to seeing you on Monday for the meeting and reading over the offer. Thanks for the opportunity and I'll talk to you later, Bailey."

"Hold on, I'll walk you out." Bailey stayed mute until we got back inside the house. "You handled that like a pro," he gushed like a little kid while we headed to the front door.

"Thanks and good looking out. This meeting would've never happened if it weren't for you. I'll never forget what you've done for me." I meant that shit too. I would joke a lot about Bailey being goofy and nerdy, but I had developed a lot of love for dude. He genuinely wanted to see me win which automatically made him a part of my team.

"You deserve it, man." That endearing goofy smile never left Bailey's face. "From the first time I heard you at that underground spot I knew big things were coming your way. You had way too much talent for it not to. I'm just happy that you're taking me along for the ride."

"Of course I'm taking you. This gonna be a long ride so prepare yourself." I winked.

"I'm ready," Bailey yelled out as I walked up the block towards the train station. "You better be ready too!" he yelled some more.

I'm ready all right, I thought to myself. I really wanted to punch my fist to the sky and scream that out at the top of my lungs so the world could hear me, but contained myself. Holding back my enthusiasm over what Clay had said was a struggle for me. I was tempted to give that motherfucker a hug when he told me that Def Jam would be making me an offer, but he started with the Jedi mind tricks so I had to play my part if I wanted to win the game.

No, I didn't have any other labels offering me a deal, but yes I was headed to the recording studio. Arnez had set it up. He felt I needed to record a demo. He said with a demo, he would then be able to start shopping my music to industry heads he was cool with. Arnez was speaking my language. I had never been in a studio before and I was ready to be behind the mic. It seemed within the last few weeks Arnez came into my life delivering on my every command without me even having to tell him what they were, like he could hear my thoughts although I knew that was impossible. I guess Arnez figured I craved the same things that every up and coming rapper wanted... to be a star.

I had been at the studio recording for over four hours and we wasn't letting up. It was a nice studio too. Not some half ass hole in the wall that a lot of no name rappers like myself start at. This place had top of the line equipment. An actual lobby with a receptionist and lounge for people to chill in while the artist and the producers were trying to make magic happen. And speaking of producers, he linked me up with Ice, a young producer who already had a few hits under his belt. Arnez wasn't even pressed about the high price for studio time. He called it a worthwhile investment. I got what Arnez was saying, but I wasn't expecting this, such a legit set up my very first time recording. Right when I thought this night couldn't get any better, J-Rock stepped into the room.

"Yo, Ice, I didn't mean to interrupt your session, but we right next door and I had to come see who was in hear spittin' so hard." I heard the words coming out of J-Rock's mouth, but my mind wasn't processing that he was talking about me.

"This kid nice right," Ice said, smiling at J-Rock.

"What label you signed wit'?" J-Rock asked me.

"Nobody yet," I replied. I hadn't mentioned to anyone about the potential Def Jam deal and I intended to keep it like that at least for now.

"That ain't gon' last long. Somebody gon' snatch you up quick." J-Rock nodded his head. "Where you from?"

"Same place as you."

"Yo, you from Queens!" J-Rock's face lit up.

"Yep."

"Word! Yo son you need to come jump on this track wit' me right now," J-Rock said sounding extra hyped.

"Are you serious?" My mind was spinning right now. There was no way that J-Rock, who was in heavy rotation on the radio right now, killin' the rap game, asked me to jump on a record wit' him. This couldn't be my life.

"Yeah, I'm serious. I don't play 'bout my music, do I, Ice?"

"Nah, he doesn't. I've worked on a couple of tracks wit' J-Rock and he wouldn't be asking you if he wasn't serious."

"I had another rapper in mind, but I think you would be a much better fit. Come on, let's do this. You ain't scared is you?" J-Rock smirked, fuckin' wit' me.

"Let's do it." I was nervous, but I wasn't fuckin' crazy. There was no way I was gonna let an opportunity like this slip through my fingers. Not only was I a fan of J-Rock's music, I respected how he was making his mark on hip hop not only that he was from Queens. I admired the dude and now we were about to cut a record together. Things were finally falling in place for me and I was ready for all of it.

Chapter Seven

Welcome To The Family

"Wait up!" I heard Bailey yell out as I was exiting the front door at school. He was running so fast I thought he was going to trip and fall. "How is it that we attend the same school, but I've been having the hardest time tracking you down," he said between huffing and puffing once he caught up to me.

"Yo, slow down and catch your breath. You got me now... you can relax." I laughed.

"It's not funny, Xavier."

"Is that a frown I see on your face? On the real I don't think I've ever seen you frown. You always got the same goofy look on yo face. What's up?" I was joking with Bailey, but dead ass serious too. He was always so happy-go-lucky, but he seemed stressed.

"Like you don't know."

"I don't know. Talk to me, Bailey."

"It's been a few weeks since you met with my brother and the other executives at Def Jam and you still haven't signed the contract. You're really making my brother look bad. Of course he's ragging on me since I'm the one who introduced you."

"Bailey, I'm sorry about that. You really looked out for me and like I told you, we're gonna always be good because of that. But I can't sign some bullshit contract because you gave me a plug. They want everything but my unborn child and giving me squat in return. I'm not signing that shit."

"Supreme, I'm sure they can renegotiate the contract. Maybe my father can help. He's an attorney."

"Yeah, and his firm represents Def Jam. That's called a conflict of interest. Listen, I've never gone to law school, but my comprehension skills are superb and there ain't no saving that contract unless they rip it up and start all over from scratch."

"So what's your plan? You can't spend the rest of your life participating in rap battles at underground clubs. Man, you have way too much talent for that. People need to hear you and I'm not talking locally. On a national level, hell international," Bailey belted with intense passion. "You deserve to be on top!"

"You're a good dude, Bailey," I said patting him on the shoulder. "But don't worry, it will all work out. But listen, I got somewhere I need to be. We'll talk later. Stop stressing, Bailey. Everything is good," I called out as he stood in the distance with a puppy dog frown still on his face.

I knew Bailey wanted me to win and so did I, but my layout had to right. At this point for as long as I had been at this, it made no sense to sign my life away for peanuts. Plus, I had two weapons working in my favor that Bailey didn't know about. Arnez's money seemed to be endless and he had no problem financing my situation. I wasn't stupid about that either. Like my mother always told me, you'll have to pay up on the front end or the back end, but you will have to pay. When and how you pay is up to you. I have every intention of paying Arnez back every dollar he invested in, but unbeknownst to him, I had no intention of ever signing with him. A paperwork deal was out the question.

My next and most lethal weapon was J-Rock. Not only did we click in our recording session, but also we bonded. It might be a Queens thing, but he was like the coolest nigga. To my amazement, he loved the record we did together so much, he was releasing it as a single and featuring it on his upcoming CD. He told me I should hear it on the radio any day now. That was huge for me and so unexpected. Since J-Rock was a partner at his indie label, he had the power to make those sort of executive decisions. But since everybody was feeling our song it didn't take much convincing on his part. Again, I hadn't told a single soul. I preferred for the song to just drop and then let word spread setting the streets on fire all by itself.

"My man, Supreme, glad you could come through on such short notice." J-Rock greeted me with our standard handshake.

"Of course. All the love you've shown me. I'm always available for you."

"Thank you, but on the real it's all you. Your talent is what caught my ear and got you here. I'm just happy I can assist another Queens nigga an opportunity to shine. But best believe whether I helped you or not it was only a matter of time before somebody flung the door open for you. You just that talented. Not only that, you got the chocolate pretty boy swag that chicks go crazy over." J-Rock and I both laughed at his last comment.

"Man, you crazy. I'm sure you got more than your fair share of female fans," I countered.

"True, but that's 'cause I got a lil' money and fame. You know I'm rough around the edges," J-Rock said stroking his scraggily beard. "My ass need to hit the gym too, but it's all good. I ain't tryna be that sexy nigga out here. You on the other hand gon' have the women and the men loving you. You a handsome dude. A man can admit that shit and not be on no funny shit. But yo' flow. You rhyme like a beast. If I wasn't such a confident nigga, I wouldn't have even released that track we did together, 'cause you killed me on my own track."

"Man, shut up wit' that." I chuckled.

"Supreme, everybody know one thing about me, I'ma real nigga. I speak the truth. I'ma fuckin' straight shooter. Let's sit down before I get to runnin' my mouth any further. I want to make comfortable," J-Rock said sitting down on the black leather couches in his office. "Can I get you something to drink? We got anything you want up in this building," he boasted.

"Nah, I'm good."

"Cool. But back to what I was saying. Ain't no bullshit over this way. I told you our song was gon' be playing on the radio and it is... right?"

"No doubt. I still ain't heard it yet, but all my people have." I laughed.

"You still ain't heard it yet?!" J-Rock's eyes got big like he didn't believe me.

"I know it's crazy. It seems like I miss it every time it comes on. The only reason I know it was just on the radio 'cause my pager start blowing up."

"That ain't cool. We gotta do something about that," J-Rock said getting super serious.

"Of course I want to hear it and I know eventually I will. It ain't nothing for you to get upset about," I tried to assure him.

"I still remember the day, time, and exactly what I was wearing the first time I heard my song on the radio. I ain't a nostalgic type nigga, but that's a special moment and you only get one."

"True... true."

"I have an interview with Hot 97 tomorrow.

You know discussing my upcoming CD and tour. I want you to come up there with me. You definitely won't miss the song 'cause they'll play it right there in your face."

"Yo, you want me to go up to Hot 97 wit' you! I'm almost fuckin' speechless. You've got to be the coolest nigga I've ever met in my life. I can't believe you doing all this for me," I said truly stunned.

"It ain't just because I'm a cool nigga, although I am." He smiled. "On the real though, I'm doing a lot of this because I want something from you."

"What could you want from me?" I questioned, thinking I had absolutely nothing to offer this man that he didn't already have.

"I want you to sign to my label. I know these motherfuckers are coming at you left and right especially now that you getting massive radio play..."

"And that's because of you," I cut in and said.

"I don't want you to think that because I did that you are obligated to sign wit' me. I know what doing that was gonna make happen. My partner told me it was a dumb business move to release that song before we signed you because everybody would be getting at you and there would be no reason for you to sign wit' us."

I listened intently to what J-Rock was saying and his partner was right. After that song hit radio, Clay had been blowing me up nonstop. He told me to disregard that previous contract as Def Jam had a new offer for me. The people who didn't have a direct contact to me was blowing up Arnez and he was trying his hardest to get papers on me, but I kept making excuses putting the shit off. It was crazy because for the last couple of years all I wanted was for a label to sign me, but now that they were all banging down my door I wasn't even pressed and that was because of J-Rock. He was giving me the outlet to have my voice heard and for the moment that was quenching my thirst.

I continued listening as J-Rock made his case. "But that's not why I put you on that record and made it my first single. I did it because it was my best song, period. When I started this rap shit it wasn't for the money 'cause I got plenty of that. Ain't no secret out here in these streets that I was gettin' that helicopter money from supplying that dope way before anybody on radio knew who the fuck J-Rock was. That's why I've been able to fund my own shit. I'm my own man."

"I feel you."

"I hope so, 'cause I got in this rap shit because I had some things I wanted to get off my chest. What better way than to speak some shit over bangin' ass beats. I'm 'bout the music. I was already hood famous so this fame shit ain't that serious. My name just reaching a broader audience. Reaching more zip codes. I'm telling you all this because I want you to understand why I dropped our record first, when you weren't even my artist. My loyalty is to the music first. That business shit gon' handle itself when you come correct. I also wanted you to know that I ain't no petty nigga. I don't mind sharing the spotlight even if yo' light shine brighter than mine."

"I appreciate you explaining all this to me, J-Rock and I..."

"Before you say anything let me finish," he said putting his hand up. "Yes, the music come first, but I know motherfuckers got to eat. I'm well aware of that. I believe in feeding my family. I want everybody to eat good. I ain't gon' be eating a prime steak and lobster while you munching on Mickey D's. I don't get down like that. Not saying I got paper like the majors or their big budgets, but I got something else that in the long run will make you a much richer man."

"What's that?" He piqued my interest.

"I want to make you a partner at the label. That means you'll own your shit. No sharing your profits wit' a hundred motherfuckers that you don't even know, it's just me, my partner Sean, and you. Again, I can't give you a huge advance like the majors, but I think you'll be more than happy with what you do get. Plus, I wanna take you out on tour with me so you'll be making immediate money from that. I'll have you in the studio ASAP to record your first album and once that drops you'll become a rich man overnight... I promise you that."

I didn't even have to think about J-Rock's proposal. "You have a deal," I said shaking his hand.

"Although I could look at you and tell you was mad young, I knew you was a smart motherfucker. Get ready to take over. You have no idea how huge you 'bout to be. Welcome to the family," J-Rock said, giving me a hug.

Chapter Eight

Price Of Loyalty

"Baby, I'm so proud of you." Never in my life did I remember my mother hugging me this tight. "You did it! Not only are you graduating from the fancy school, you're graduating with honors just like you promised me."

"I told you I would." I gave her a slight smile like it was no big deal. Honestly, to me it really wasn't. School was never difficult for me. What was difficult was continuing to go when I knew a diploma would play no role in the career I planned to establish for myself. But I made a promise to my mother and I had no intentions of breaking it because I knew that would break her heart.

Even with my song with J-Rock on heavy rotation on the radio and all her friends, family, and co-workers congratulating her about it, none of that compared to me graduating. I could do no wrong in her eyes because of that. I hadn't even told her about me signing and being a partner with J-Rock. I decided to wait on that and let her enjoy this moment. She still thought I was going to college. I didn't want to shatter that dream until after graduation.

"Son, you did good." My dad stepped forward hugging me after my mother finally let me go.

"Thanks, Dad."

"I always knew you could accomplish anything you put your mind to. Once you finish college you'll be able to get a great job and make a good living for yourself."

I simply nodded my head like I was in agreement with what my dad was saying. His idea of a great job and mine were on complete opposite sides of the spectrum so was what we defined good living to be. But it wasn't my dad's fault. He had never stepped foot in a crib like the one Bailey and his family lived in. Once I got a glimpse of how real rich motherfuckers were doing it that was the only type of good living I aspired to achieve.

"Thanks again, Dad. I look at both of you and I see how proud you all are. I hope no matter what decisions I make in life the two of you will always be proud of me and give me your support.

"Of course, Xavier. We love and support you no matter what. Now give me another hug," my mother said, getting misty eyed.

"Ma, don't you dare start crying. Then you gon' make me cry and you know I'm already late for this get together Tyreek having."

"I'm sorry, baby. You go ahead." My mom released me from her embrace. She started wiping away a couple of tears that escaped her eyes. I could only imagine how she was going to be the day of my graduation.

"Have fun, son!" my dad yelled out as I was walking out the door.

"I will, Dad!" I yelled back. As I was closing the door I felt my pager vibrating. It was Arnez. I had been dodging him for the last couple of weeks, but we did need to talk. I had J-Rock hold off on making any sort of announcement about our deal because I wanted to let Arnez know first. I had so much going on, I kept putting that conversation on the back burner, but I couldn't do that any longer. It was time for me to come clean with Arnez and I planned on doing so this week.

"Yo what up, man!" Tyreek high-fived me and handed me a drink when I arrived at the lounge he was having the get-together.

"How long this spot been here?" I asked looking around at all the silver and white décor. It had a sleek yet intimate feel to it.

"It's new. It's been open for about a month."

"Place is nice," I commented glancing over at the all-glass bar.

"Damn sure is and it wasn't cheap neither to rent out this spot. But you only graduate once."

"What, this is... a graduation party? Nigga, you dropped out two years ago."

"I know! I would've graduated this year if I stayed in school. But all my friends graduating." Tyreek smiled. It's only right we celebrate."

"Man, you so crazy." I couldn't help but love Tyreek. Only his crazy ass would throw a graduation party with no diploma. Like many of the dudes in our neighborhood, he had dropped out of school and was now selling drugs. It was hard for them to bypass that easy money. "So where everybody at?"

"I kept the guest list small. Can't have a bunch of fools up in here. But everybody in the other room drinking, smoking, and shit. Follow me. Let me lead the way," Tyrek's drunk ass said.

When we got to the other room it was maybe a dozen people over there, all local friends from the neighborhood. I was feeling the vibe. It was very laid back and chill.

"You made it." Isaac came up to me cheesing.

"I told you I was coming."

"But you big time now. Song all on the radio, up on Hot 97 with J-Rock, wasn't sure if you had time for us regular folks," Isaac joked.

"Whatever, nigga."

"I'm glad you came through. Come over here for a sec, I want you to meet somebody," Isaac said being extra cheerful.

"A'ight." I grabbed another drink on my way trailing behind Isaac.

"X, I want you to meet my girlfriend, Melanie." It wasn't until she turned around did I realize what Melanie this was. "Baby, this is Xavier. You probably know him as Supreme though. Melanie couldn't believe that my best friend was the rapper Supreme." Isaac grinned.

"Xavier, I've heard so much about you. As much as Isaac talks about you I feel like I already know you." Melanie made the comment like this was the very first time she had ever seen my face. I never pegged her as an actress but the way she was playing this so laid back and nonchalant that's exactly what she was. I decided to play right along.

"I'm sure you do. So how long you and Melanie been together? You never mentioned you had a girlfriend," I said casually.

"We've been dating for a few months now, but Melanie was only ready to make it official a week ago. She wanted to keep everything low key until she knew I was the one," Isaac stated and even though the lights were dim, I swear this nigga was blushing.

"Yeah, Isaac proved he was the only guy for me. I'm so lucky to have him and I couldn't be happier," Melanie added, gently caressing the side of Isaac's cheek.

"I'm the lucky one," Isaac then said kissing Melanie on the lips as he stroked his fingers through her short tapered jet black hair. She had his nose wide open and he loved that shit.

"Baby, will you go get me another drink pretty please," Melanie purred then nibbled on Isaac's ear.

"Sure will." Isaac smiled. "X, can I get you something?" he then turned to me and asked.

"Nah, I'm good."

"Cool, I'll be right back. Ya'll get to know each other while I'm gone." Isaac was still grinning from ear to ear as he headed off to get Melanie another drink.

"Isn't he sweet." Melanie stated in a mischievous voice.

"I never realized how conniving you are until now," I said shaking my head.

"That's what you get for not paying attention to me. If you had you would've known conniving is only one of my personality traits," Melanie said proudly.

"This is what the bullshit is about... that I don't pay attention to you? 'Cause it definitely ain't no love connection wit' Isaac since you were just sucking my dick less than a week ago. What the fuck are you doing?"

"Oh, are you jealous Xavier, or should I call you Supreme." Melanie then reached down as if trying to put her hands down my pants.

"Get yo' fuckin' hands away from me!" I snarled, pushing her arm away. "Hell no, I ain't jealous, but I am pissed that you've sucked my friend into some juvenile game you playing. I think Isaac needs to know what sort of trick his new girlfriend is."

"You wouldn't dare. But even if you did, Isaac would hate you for it. Whatever story I spin is the one he'll believe. You know what my sex game is like. He was a virgin you know. I was his first. Broke him in real good. Isaac is sprung and there is nothing you can do about it."

"Yo, you're so fuckin' foul."

"Fuck you, Xavier! You think you such hot shit 'cause you on the radio. You never thought I was good enough for you. Only wanted to check for me when you wanted to bust a nut. Well now I with your friend and he appreciates me so deal with it."

"Sorry, I took so long but Tyreek was talking my head off at the bar," Isaac explained, handing Melanie her glass. "Tyreek is drunk as fuck." Isaac laughed.

"Yeah, he was already lit when I got here. I can only imagine how drunk he is now," I said ready to get away from Isaac and Melanie, but for two different reasons. The more I looked at the two of them standing next to each other, the more I wanted to tell Isaac to leave Melanie alone because she was poison. But something held me back. I think it was because part of me believed what Melanie said was true. Isaac would hate me if I knocked his new girlfriend off the pedestal he unwisely put her on.

"So how are my best friend and girl getting along?" I had never seen Isaac this happy. I guess finally getting some pussy had him floating.

"We're getting along real good." Melanie spoke in this sweet, innocent voice.

"Yep, she seems like cool people," I lied. "I'll be back. I'ma go check on Tyreek."

"That's a good idea." Isaac nodded.

"It was nice meeting you," I heard Melanie say in that same fake sugary voice.

I didn't even stop and have a conversation with Tyreek, instead I walked right out the door. Melanie had ruined my night. I couldn't believe I didn't see her for the trifling chick she was. It was probably because the relationship was never that deep for me. It was strictly about casual sex, but Isaac was way too strung to understand that. We had been friends since we were kids and I was not about to let silly ass Melanie ruin that. I was done dealing with her ever again and hopefully Isaac would eventually realize on this own that she was not the one for him.

"I was beginning to think we weren't friends anymore," Arnez said when I arrived at the diner we would frequent on occasion in the city.

"Never that. You've done too much for me. I'll always consider you a friend. These last few weeks have been crazy, that's all."

"Been hanging out with J-Rock. Recently graduated from high school. Speaking of graduation, I got something for you."

"What's this?" I questioned, looking at the small box.

"Open it," Arnez responded.

"Wow, a Rolex watch. This is nice. Very nice."

"Put it on," Arnez insisted.

"I can't."

"What you mean you can't."

"I can't take this, Arnez. You've already done enough for me. It's time I did something for you," I said, handing Arnez an envelope.

Arnez opened the envelope and I could see his eyes widen. He then looked up at me and then back down at the envelope. "How much is in here?"

"More than enough to cover all the money you've spent on me, plus extra. It's my way of saying thanks."

"How did you come into all this money?"

"J-Rock," I admitted

"J-Rock is giving you this sort of cash. Why would he do that unless..."

"Unless I signed with his label, which I did."

"Why the fuck would you sign with a bullshit label like J-Rock's? You could've signed with anybody and got a shitload more than what's in this fuckin' envelope," he barked, slamming the envelope down on the table.

"J-Rock made me an offer I couldn't refuse."

"What the fuck could that be?"

"A partnership. I'm an equal partner with him and Sean in Platinum Records. Besides that, he did give me a hefty advance. More than enough so I could pay you back with plenty left. Most importantly, I'm about to start recording my album ASAP and I'll be able to do it my way."

"I guess you got this shit all figured out huh. I knew you were smart, but I never pegged you as slick."

"I understand you might feel some kinda way that I signed the deal with J-Rock without discussing it with you, but it was nothing personal."

"That's where you're wrong. It's very personal. You always knew you had no intention of signing a management deal with me."

"Arnez, I was always upfront about wanting to take my time to sign papers with anybody, including you."

"But you had no problem letting me spend

my money on clothes, jewelry, studio time, and any other shit you wanted."

"And I paid you back every dime and then some."

"You can't put no price on all the shit I did for you. I found you on a corner block rapping for free. I put you on and you show your gratitude by signing a deal with another motherfucker. You're smart, but too dumb to understand what the price of loyalty is." Arnez took his money, the watch, and then stormed out.

Chapter Nine

New Beginnings

I've heard stories about overnight success, but never believed it. I figured people never saw all the behind the scene work that went into the success materializing. But now that it was on the verge of happening to me, I had an entirely different view. I know to me it felt like it took forever to get put on. But never for one second did I imagine my life would do a 180 like it was about to do in a few short months. Little by little, it seemed Xavier was being phased out until he no longer existed and Supreme was completely taking over. There were only two people fighting for Xavier to stay present, but they were about to lose that battle.

"Xavier, what is going on with college? You said you were going to NYU, but I haven't seen any books and I know classes already started. Did something happen with the scholarship and you didn't want to tell me and your father?" my mother asked.

"No."

"Then what is going on?"

"I haven't been going to school and I have no intentions of attending NYU."

"You're not making any sense. But you're never home. If you haven't been going to school then where have you been going?" My mother's face was filled with confusion. This wasn't how I originally planned to break the news to her, but I had procrastinated telling the truth long enough.

"I've been in the studio recording my album."

"Your album... what album?"

"My solo album. I got a record deal, Ma."

"A record deal with who?"

"Platinum Records. They're an independent record label, but I'm a part owner. So I won't be going to college."

"You gave up a full scholarship to NYU to sign with some unknown record label! Are you crazy!" my father barked. He popped out of nowhere. I didn't even know he was home. I would've never came clean with my mother right now if I knew my father was lurking around the corner.

"J-Rock is a successful artist and he's confident that I'm going to blow up once my album drops. He already had me do a few local shows with him and I made good money and next month he wants me to go out on tour."

"You're ready to throw away your entire life to pursue some rap career. I thought we were past that, Xavier. After you went to that prep school I was under the impression you had your head screwed on tight, boy was I wrong." My father shook his head in disgust.

"My head is screwed on perfectly fine. The only reason I went to that school was to make Mom happy. I never stopped pursuing my rap career. And so you know, I could've signed with just about any label I wanted, but I chose Platinum Records because not only am I an artist, I'm also a partner at the label. I'm part of something bigger than just my music. I have control over my fate."

"You don't have control over nothing. You're relying on a bunch of finicky customers to either make or break your career. Just because you got some song playing on the radio doesn't mean they're going to go out and buy your music. Going to college guarantees you getting a good job with a steady income. What you're doing now guarantees you squat," my dad barked.

"Dad, I'm sorry you feel that way, but I won't apologize for my decision to pursue my rap career instead of attending college. Nothing in life is guaranteed, including getting a degree that lands you a great job and making good money. But even if it did, I would still pass. I rather fail at something I love doing then succeed at something I hate."

"Supreme, neither me or your father want you to be unhappy. We're only concerned about your future and want you to be practical."

"Stop babying him," my dad snapped at my mom. "Xavier, if you don't plan on attending college then you can't live here."

"You don't mean that!" my mother said, looking at my father.

"Yes, I do," my dad stated firmly.

"This is our home," my mom emphasized the word our. "You can't make a decision like that on your own. Xavier has every right to live here. This is his home too."

"Not if he's not attending school."

"I understand you're upset about him not attending college. I'm not happy about it either, but you're taking this too far. I can't—"

"Mom, it's okay. I don't have to stay here. I can move out. The last thing I want to do is cause problems between the two of you." I started packing up my stuff.

"Xavier, please don't go," my mom begged as we watched my dad walk out the door. "Your dad will calm down. He's upset right now, but please don't leave."

"Mom, he isn't going to change his mind. We both know how he is and honestly it's okay."

"But where will you go?"

"I have money. I might stay with Tyreek or Isaac for a couple days until I can find a more permanent situation, but I'll be fine. It's time for me to get out and be on my own anyway. Don't worry." I hugged my mother wanting to reassure her that I would be fine.

"Please call me and stay in touch. I don't want to lose you."

"That will never happen. I'ma call you. I promise. Do you mind if I come back tomorrow while you and dad are at work to get the rest of my stuff?"

"Of course I don't mind. This is still your home, it always will be." My mother held on to me so tightly like she was afraid to let me go. I had spent the last eighteen years of my life in this house and I was ready for a new beginning.

"I can't believe my album is finally done! In less than thirty minutes this studio will be completely filled for my listening party. Life is good!" I smiled unable to contain my excitement. But the thing is I didn't want to. I wanted to relish in this moment for as long as possible.

"You did it, man. Proud of you," J-Rock said giving me a brotherly embrace. "Your single is already in the top ten with a bullet going up. Once this album is released and the video we just shot drops, you gon' be outta here.

"Everything you said would happen is coming true. I'm still having a hard time believing this is my life."

"It is and you deserve all the good fortune that's coming your way. You spent endless nights in the studio recording your album making sure it was done just right. This CD will go down as a classic. You've solidified yourself in this rap game. Mark my words."

"Damn, J-Rock, that means a lot coming from

you. I felt I had a lot to prove so I definitely gave it my all."

"It shows. But we about to have a lot of industry heads, media, and of course some of your friends so let's get ready." J-Rock appeared to be equally if not more hyped about tonight.

As the people started flowing in, this euphoric energy took over my body. Even when Isaac showed up with Melanie my good mood remained on ten. It only got better when Bailey arrived. He always believed I could go far even before the deal. It was only right that he be here to hear my album played for the very first time.

"Can I get everybody's attention!" J-Rock announced standing in front of the room. "Thank you all for coming to share what I can honestly say is one of the best moments of my life. I know this ain't my album, but I got so much love for this young brother that I feel like it is. He's part of my family and I believe without a doubt this is a classic and will go down in history as one of the best hip hop albums ever made and I'm proud to be a part of that. I present for your listening pleasure, what I'm predicting right now will debut at number one, my partner and artist's debut album, fittingly dubbed Supreme."

Everyone applauded as the lights dimmed and the first track 'Infamous,' echoed through the speakers. I closed my eyes and let the words I spoke marinate in my mind. Song after song told a story of life not only mine, but those of so many that I had known. When the song 'Venomous' came on I heard a bunch of ooh's and aah's as I spit lyrics about a trifling female who eventually ends up getting played.

As I spit each lyric the people in attendance got more hyped. I looked around to take in everyone's expression. I tried to quickly turn away when my eyes locked with Melanie. She had the look of death on her face. I couldn't help but laugh because I knew her silly ass probably thought the song was about her. I sat back in my chair and continued listening to the final tracks, enjoying the music along with everyone else.

When the lights came back on I was surprised to see Arnez holding court in the back. It was the first time I had seen him since our altercation at the diner. I saw him get up, but before I had a chance to go over and say something to him, Bailey came running over. He wanted to be the first to congratulate me.

"I'm almost speechless and you know that never happens to me." Bailey hit me with that same pig snort that I had grown to appreciate. "To this day my brother still hates me because you didn't sign with Def Jam. He's going to really hate me after this CD drops because you're about to be huge, even bigger than I imagined. Thank you for letting me be a part of this."

"It wouldn't be the same without you, Bailey."

"You did that, X!" Isaac was cheesing hard. "J-Rock is right, that's classic material right there. As always I'm proud of you, man."

"Thanks, Isaac. Glad you were here to share this moment with me. But can you all excuse me for a minute. I need to use the restroom," I said hurrying off. I needed to use the bathroom hours ago, but I think my excitement for this listening party made me put it off. Right after I finished and was zipping up my jeans I heard the door opening and Arnez walked in.

"I didn't mean to intrude, but I wanted to talk to you in private and when I saw you headed to the bathroom I took advantage of the opportunity."

"No problem," I said washing my hands. "I will admit I was shocked to see you here. I didn't even know you were aware that I was having my listening party tonight."

"You know I have some connections in the industry. I wanted to be one of the first to hear what all the buzz was about. I can't lie, you made good on your promise to bring the heat. Your fans will not be disappointed, Supreme."

"And you, are you disappointed that you won't be eatin' off this album?"

"Of course I am. I'm a businessman, but I also like you as a person, Supreme, and I was looking forward to us working together. But these last few months I've had time to do a lot of thinking. I was pissed at you or more so pissed at myself for mixing my personal feelings with business. I know better than that and I won't make that mistake again. I've learned from it and there's no reason why we still can't be cool."

"I would like that, Arnez. Like I told you, you were instrumental in a lot of this shit happening for me and I'll always be grateful for that."

"I can see you're being sincere and that makes this situation easier for me to accept. I always knew you were talented. Having a front row seat as your star shines is an incredible feeling. I hope I can continue to be a part of that and keep my front row seat."

"I would like that."

"To new beginnings," Arnez stated reaching out his hand.

"Yes, to new beginnings." We shook hands and a feeling of relief came over me knowing that the beef I had with Arnez had been squashed.

"I'm not going to hold you up any longer. But I'll be in touch," Arnez said.

"Looking forward to it." When the door closed behind Arnez I took a long look in the mirror. The reflection staring back at me was one I was proud of. Tonight was a new beginning for me in so many ways. I washed my hands one more time and dried them off and to my dismay when I exited the bathroom I was greeted with the last person I wanted to see.

"Mothefucker, I know that song you recorded was about me. How dare you rap about me without giving me proper compensation." Melanie was standing in front of me with her arms firmly folded over her black jumpsuit and lips poked out like she had every right to have an attitude.

"Yo, you need to chill. Now can you move out my way?" Melanie was blocking my path and I was trying to not put hands on her.

"I ain't going nowhere until you give me what you owe," she said not budging. To avoid a confrontation, I walked around Melanie, but instead of her letting me walk away she grabbed my arm.

"Don't do that," I said calmly.

"I can do whatever the fuck I want to do! You don't run nothing this way!"

"What are you so hostile about? That song wasn't about you. You ain't the only triflin' girl I know."

"Whatever, nigga. You know that song is about me. Stop actin' like you don't miss this pussy," Melanie said, stroking her long nails across my cheek."

"Yo, you're seriously delusional."

"Fuck you, Xavier! Get your hands off of me. I'm with Isaac. I don't want you!" Melanie yelled then turned around and slapped the shit out of me.

"What the fuck is wrong wit' you!" I belted snatching her arm.

"Leave her alone!" Isaac roared jumping on my back. It took me a second to process that my best friend and his lowdown girlfriend was tag teaming me at my own fuckin' listening party.

"Isaac, get off of me, man!" I barked flipping him off my back.

"Baby, are you okay," Melanie screamed out, bending over next to Isaac who was now picking himself up off the floor.

"I'm fine," he mumbled getting up. "X, what is wrong wit' you? You can have any girl you want. Why you gotta go after mine." I could see the hurt in Isaac's eyes and all that did was make me even more mad.

"I can't believe you think I would be coming after yo' girl. I don't want Melanie."

"He's lying, Isaac."

"Man, I saw what happened with my own eyes."

"No, you saw what this silly broad wanted you to see," I said, pointing my finger at Melanie. "She was waiting for me when I came out the bathroom, swearing down that one of the tracks on my album was about her. I told her she was wrong and then she started stroking my face and I guess when she saw you walking up she flipped it to make it seem like I was coming on to her. "

"Don't believe anything he's saying, Isaac. If you want to know the truth, I used to date Xavier. But as his music career started taking off he took me for granted. Then I met you and we fell in love. When we were at Tyreek's party that was the first time Xavier saw us together, although I had told him we were a couple. He was furious. I guess that's why he made that song 'Venomous' about me. Then when I confronted him about it he tried to come on to me. He actually asked me to come in the bathroom and give him some head."

"Yo, this lying trick can't be serious!" I scoffed throwing my hands up.

"Shut up, X!" Isaac barked. I was staring at him stunned that he was falling for Melanie's bullshit story.

"Baby, I know I should've been honest with you, but I didn't want to ruin your friendship with

Xavier. I know how close you are. Can you please forgive me," Melanie pleaded and even started crying to make this performance she was putting on more believable.

"Isaac, can't you see she's lying. She's trying to play you," I tried to reason with him.

"Then answer this one question."

"What is it?"

"Did you used to mess around with Melanie?"

I let out a deep sigh and put my head down. "Yes, but it wasn't like that. I know I shoulda told you but..."

"But nothing. How am I supposed to believe anything you say about Melanie when you weren't even honest to me about your dealings with her? You're so used to always winning everything especially when it comes to me that you couldn't deal that for the first time a girl chose me over you. That's really fucked up, Supreme."

"Isaac, it wasn't like that. I swear man. You're like a brother to me. I would never do no foul shit to you like that." But Isaac wasn't trying to hear nothing I had to say. His eyes were filled with so much hate. Never did I think a guy I grew up with and knew for most of my life would ever look at me that way. Isaac and Melanie left the building holding hands leaving a piece of me broken, and my night ruined.

Chapter Ten

Making Things Right

If every prediction made about me was destined to come true then they had. Not sure if it was J-Rock or me that spoke it into existence or a combination of both, but I was now a part of the overnight success club. My debut album "Supreme" shot straight to number one. I also had the number one song in the country. Then the track 'Venomous' that we had no intention of releasing as a single also hit the Billboard Charts after radio start giving it heavy airplay. Life was so lovely for me right now that it scared me. Sometimes things could be just too perfect.

"You ready for the show tonight?" J-Rock asked as we sat in the offices of Platinum Records bullshitting before our concert that night.

"After all the shows we've done you would think I wouldn't be nervous, but New York is my city. All my people will be there tonight. Well almost all my people," I said my voice trailing off.

"Still no word from Isaac?"

"Nope. I left him a few messages at home and I even left a message with his moms. I was hoping he would've gotten in touch with me by now."

"It's still early enough for him to get in touch with you. Don't get up in yo' feelings yet." J-Rock chuckled.

"Man, I haven't spoken to him since that trifling trick lied on me at my listening party. I knew I shoulda come clean wit' him the second I found out he was fuckin' wit' her. I guess I was hoping he would realize on his own that Melanie wasn't about shit and cut her loose, but that hoe got her nails dug deep in that nigga."

"When a female got a nigga open off some pussy, you gotta fall back and let that shit play the fuck out. 'Cause he gon' always choose that pussy over you. Don't take the shit personally. You know a motherfucka don't even start gettin' halfway good sense until he around twenty-five. Hell, I been past twenty-five and my good sense only kick in every once in a while."

"Nigga, you is crazy," I said as we both laughed. "I've known Isaac damn near all my life. He like family so I'm not giving up on him."

"And you shouldn't, but if—"

"Hold on!" I spoke out loudly. "Maybe Isaac hasn't given up on me neither." I smiled looking at my pager.

"That's him?" J-Rock asked. I nodded my head letting him know it was. "I told you that nigga would eventually call. He probably finally got from sniffing behind that girl."

"Let me call him," I said picking up the office phone.

"What's up! I wasn't expecting for you to call me so quick," Isaac said when he answered the phone.

"I guess I was surprised to hear from you and glad. How you been?"

"I've been doing a'ight. I would ask how you been, but I know you doing good. Congrats on the success of your album."

"Thank you, man. Not sure if you got my

messages or not, but we have a show at Madison Square Garden tonight."

"Yeah, I heard. That's all everybody in Queens talkin' 'bout."

"I still got them tickets and some backstage passes if you wanna come."

"I appreciate that, but it's so last minute and I don't have anybody to go with."

"Bailey is coming and I don't think he's bringing anybody. You can hang wit' him. You know he'll like that." I laughed. "He's actually meeting me here at Platinum records and riding over to the venue with me. If you can get over here before five you can ride wit' us too."

"You sure?"

"Positive. It'll be like old times us hanging out. So you coming?"

"Yeah, I'll be there."

This feeling of relief came over me. I felt like I had my brother back. "Cool, write this down," I said giving Isaac the address to the record label before hanging up.

"From that big ass smile on your face, I guess that means Isaac will be up in the building," J-Rock cracked.

"Yep, you were right. You might be right about him gettin' from up under Melanie's ass.'"

"Nigga, I'm always right," J-Rock stated

matter of factly. "But seriously, why you think that?"

"I told him I had two tickets to the show for him, but at first he declined. He said it was last minute and didn't have anyone to go with. If he was still with Melanie I would think he would bring her."

"True or maybe he might not want her to know you cool again. But none of that shit matter." J-Rock shrugged, flinging his hand.

"You right. None of that matter. I got my brother back. All that other shit will work itself out."

"You right about that," J-Rock agreed, reaching for a cigarette.

I glanced down at my watch to see how much time I had. "Let me get outta here."

"Where you going?"

"To meet wit' my parents for a second. I won't be gone that long. I'll definitely be back before Bailey and Isaac get here."

"I'll be here chillin' so take your time in case they get here before you back. Just don't miss the show."

"I ain't missing that show at Madison Square Garden. Is you crazy!"

"You bet not. I know you done sold more albums in your first week then I have thus far, but you still my opening act," J-Rock reminded me in a funny way. "So don't be late."

"I'll be back." I shook my head laughing to myself about what J-Rock said then headed out.

I arrived to 3621 Berkshire Court first. I waited in the driveway checking the rearview to see when my parents arrived. I turned on the radio while waiting and heard the commercial for the official after party J-Rock and I were hosting tonight for the concert. My life had done a one 180 in a year and I still kept thinking that any day I might wake up from my dream. The thing was when I opened my eyes every morning my life was only getting better.

"Thank you." I looked up and said. Right then I saw my mom and dad pulling up. I jumped out and they seemed so startled. "Hey! You didn't have a hard time finding this place did you?"

"A little," my mom answered as my dad clearly didn't want to admit it.

"We're here," my dad managed to say slamming the car door.

"Come give me a hug," my mom beamed. "I haven't seen you in so long."

"You know I've been on tour," I said missing her embrace. My mom always felt so warm and full of love.

"I know, but that didn't stop me from missing you." She squeezed me tight and I could smell she was wearing the perfume I got for her when we had a stop in LA. J-Rock took me to some swanky ass store in Beverly Hills and I knew my mother would love it. The store mailed it directly to her. She called me so excited. My mom had no idea how good that made me feel.

"So why did you want us to meet you here?" my dad questioned ending my reflective moment. "You wanted to show off one of your celebrity friend's fancy houses?

"Actually I wanted to show you your new house."

"What!" my mother yelled out. She was so loud I almost jumped. My father stood there with his mouth halfway open and he was never at a lost for words.

"Say that again?" he finally managed to mutter.

"I bought this house for the two of you. Here are they keys. Why don't you go in...." before I could complete my sentence my mother broke down and started crying.

"I can't believe you did this for us. We don't deserve it," she cried out.

"Don't ever say that. Of course you deserve it." I pulled my mom in for a hug.

"Son, I don't know what to say. I'm shocked. I figured you were making money, but nothing that could afford you this," my dad mumbled in disbelief looking at the five bedroom, six bath, five thousand square foot custom built home.

"Let's just say this music has been good to me and of course I want to share it with the ones I love the most." I caught my dad's eyes tearing up. He tried his best not to let one drop escape. I had a very complicated relationship with my dad, but it didn't negate how much I loved him. But honestly, I bought this house for my mother. She always did her best to keep the love flowing in our house and for that she deserved the world.

"My baby." My mom kept shaking her head. "When I carried you in my stomach I knew you were special. When I gave birth to you, I told God you were perfect. But with everything inside of me never in my life did I imagine my baby, who at the age of nineteen would be giving me the keys to my very own house and a house like this. Thank you."

"You're more than welcome. You believed in my dreams and me. Now I want to fulfill all your dreams. Now we can celebrate together. Me opening up at Madison Square Garden and the two of you being the owners of a brand new house. Now let's go inside and take a look around because I have a show to do and you all have a show to attend." We all hugged it out and headed inside.

Chapter Eleven

I Rise You Fall

I was rushing to get back to the office. Luckily traffic was light. My parents didn't want to leave their new crib. I couldn't blame them. I knew I should have waited and given them the keys on a day that wasn't so hectic, but I wanted this day to represent something memorable for all of us. When I finally pulled up to the front of Platinum Records, I was a little late, but we were still good on time. I noticed that the limos and SUV's that would be transporting everyone to the Garden weren't out front.

"I guess I'm not the only one running late." I laughed getting out my car. I figured J-Rock went from smoking cigarettes to lighting blunts and lost track of time. I took the elevator upstairs and wondered did J-Rock have Bailey and Isaac in there smoking too. When the elevator doors opened it was eerily quiet. I wasn't expecting any staff to be in the building as most of them were probably already at the Garden, but with J-Rock, Bailey, Isaac, and security being there I thought it would be a little more lively.

"Damn, did them niggas leave without me?" I questioned out loud. I glanced down at my pager to see if I missed any calls, but there was nothing. "I bet them motherfuckers already left. I should've went straight there," I grumbled getting annoyed with myself. I needed to stop back in the lounge and get my duffel bag because I assumed J-Rock didn't think to take it with him before they left.

As I walked down the hall, I heard my pager go off. It was Isaac's number. "Damn, I guess he didn't make it here after all. I'll call him in a second," I said out loud opening the door to the lounge, but it seemed jammed for a second. I turned the knob again, but had to shove hard as if something was pressed against it.

Then it happened. That dream I had been living had turned into a nightmare in a matter of seconds. There was J-Rock still sitting in the same chair as when I left, but this time half his face was blown off. Two of our security guards were both face down on the floor with their bodies riddled with bullets. "Damn! Not you too Bailey." I kneeled down looking at his dead body leaning against the door. I didn't know if I wanted to cry, vomit, or walk back out the building and pretend that if I walked back in I would realize that this was all just a figment of my imagination. But it wasn't. Four people that I had nothing but love for were all dead and my life would never be the same again.

It had been two weeks since I walked into a bloody massacre and I spent those two weeks attending four different funerals and speaking to the police. They didn't have any leads and my life seemed like it was at a standstill.

"I find myself sitting in here a lot too," I heard Sean say, snapping me out of my thoughts.

"Yeah, for some reason I feel the most connected to J-Rock when I'm in his office sitting behind his desk."

"I feel you. I keep thinking I'm gonna walk in here and he'll start telling me one of his silly ass jokes. There's just no way my man can be dead." Sean sat down on the couch and put his head down. They had been running the streets together since they were kids so I knew Sean was beyond fucked up.

"All I want to know is who... who did this. I won't be able to move forward until I get the answer to that question."

"Man, the police are saying it was a robbery gone bad. All of J-Rock's jewelry was missing and cash. If that's the case we may not ever find out who's responsible," Sean stated.

"Why you say that?"

"They're so many crews that do nothing but sit around plotting on how to rob rich niggas. They be at the recording studios and tend to hit independent labels because they're an easier target than the bigger labels. What's so crazy is that just a week before this shit happened, J-Rock and me was discussing setting up an appointment to have some surveillance cameras installed. If we had we would know who killed him." Sean sighed.

"That shit don't even matter 'cause we gon find out who's responsible. I won't make another record until I do. I don't have a choice. J-Rock is a big reason why I'm in the position I'm in today. If I don't find out who did this, I'll feel like I let him down."

"Supreme, don't think like that. I remember the first time J-Rock told me about you. His exact words were, 'that kid got it. He gon' surpass me on every level and I ain't even mad 'cause I like the kid.' He might've given you that extra push, but you were destined to be a star with or without J-Rock."

"Maybe, but I don't care. That could've easily been me in that lounge with half my face blown off. If it had, I know J-Rock would do everything in his power to find my killer. I owe him the same thing."

"I feel you, but J-Rock wouldn't want you to put your life or career on hold to do so. The two of us are partners in Platinum records. We owe it to J-Rock to finish what he started. He would turn in his grave if we let this label crumble."

I was thinking about what Sean said, but my mind was consumed on getting revenge on the people responsible for taking away the person who in a lot of ways I thought of as a mentor. The only reason why at the age of nineteen I was already rich was because J-Rock convinced me to become a partner in my own label instead of signing with someone else and being simply an artist. He opened my eyes to not only utilizing my skills as a rapper, but also as a businessperson. Then there was Bailey. A good kid whose only crime was being at the wrong place at the wrong time. He wasn't even about this life and it cost him his. The only positive thing I can think of, is that Isaac had got held up and wasn't able to make it. If he had gotten killed too, I don't think I would've ever been able to forgive myself.

"You right, Sean. J-Rock would want Platinum Records to flourish and we're going to make sure that people never forget he will always be a part of this label."

"Do you have something in mind?"

"Yep. If I'ma get back in the studio, it's gonna be for a purpose. My next album is going to be called The Legacy Of J-Rock. Each track will be about him in some way."

"Yo that's dope, Supreme. J-Rock would love that. When you gon' get started?"

"ASAP. All this anger and pain I'm feeling. I'ma release it in my music. This will be by far the best form of therapy for me." I looked up at the picture on the wall of J-Rock and me. We were holding the platinum plaque for my debut album

'Supreme'. That was one of the happiest days of our lives and this was one of my saddest.

"Thanks so much for coming by," Isaac's mom said when she opened the door.

"Of course. We family," I said giving Ms. Crawford a hug. "I haven't been over here in so long, but it still feels like home." I smiled remembering all the times I spent in this house playing with Isaac.

"This will always be your home." Ms. Crawford tried to give me a smile, but I could see all the pain in her eyes. I was hoping what she told me over the phone wasn't true, but their was no denying her anguish.

"Where's Isaac?"

"Upstairs in his room. Isaac doesn't know you're here. I thought it best to not tell him you were coming. He might've left. He wouldn't want you to see him like this."

"I understand. I'll go upstairs and talk to him."

Ms. Crawford stopped me before I headed up the stairs and gave me another hug. "Thank you again for coming. I know how busy you are and for you to make time for us just goes to show that everyone doesn't let fame go to their heads." She kissed me on the cheek and let me go.

I walked slowly up the stairs dreading the conversation I was about to have with Isaac. I knocked on his bedroom door and when he told me to come in, I barely recognized the person I had considered to be a brother.

"X, what you doin' here!" he questioned becoming extra jittery. He jumped off his bed and he had this wild crazy look in his eyes. He had extremely small pinpoint pupils and he had lost so much weight that his face was sunken in. The last time I saw him was at Bailey's funeral three months ago and now he was looking like what he was, a dope fiend. I was still holding out hope that his mom was wrong, but the visual put that to rest.

"I came to check on you."

"You didn't have to do that. I'm good," he lied reaching for a long sleeve shirt to cover the cuts and scabs on his arms, but I had already seen enough.

"Isaac man, what happened? Just a few months ago you were in school, had a job, even your own apartment. Now..." my voice trailed off.

"Nah... nah... nah, it's nothin' like that, X. I'm good. You didn't have to come all this way. I'm sure you got a show or something to do. Don't worry about me," Isaac said scratching his arm.

Looking at Isaac I couldn't wrap my mind around how shit went so bad so fast for him. I wondered how long he had been using and how he was able to hide his addiction up until recently.

"I want you to go to rehab and I'll pay for the treatment. I can't let you do this to yourself."

"Why do you even care," Isaac said nodding off. That quick his mood had changed from jittery to slow moving and lethargic.

"How you even ask me that. We brothers, man. I would do anything for you."

"Just get outta here! I don't want yo' help. I wanna be left alone."

"So you can do more drugs. You better than that, Isaac, and yo' mom deserves better than that. You breakin' that woman's heart."

"I know man," Isaac wept. He then began sobbing uncontrollably. I didn't understand what was going on with him, but his emotions were running deep.

"Let me help you, Isaac. You don't have to go through this alone." Although I hated to mention her name, but I had to question if his depressed state was due to Melanie. His mom told me they broke up not too long ago and I wondered if that breakup pushed him over the edge.

"There's no helping me," Isaac continued to sob.

"Does this depression you seem to be in have anything to do with you and Melanie breaking up?"

Isaac turned away and put his head down. I pressed on because I figured I must be on to something. "There are plenty of other girls in this world besides Melanie. Once we get you cleaned up and your life back in order it won't be hard to find you a replacement. You can even come work with me over at the label. Get you a good salary with benefits. Life will be good," I said with enthusiasm.

"I can't let you do that."

"I want to. We family."

"X, you don't get it."

"Get what?"

Isaac's whimper were now getting louder and lasted longer and longer. This feeling of helplessness was eating me up. "Isaac, just tell me what I can do so we can make this shit right! I can't watch you destroy your life like this."

"My life is over."

"Stop saying bullshit like that. Yo' life ain't fuckin' over," I barked.

"My life ended on May 16th." I deliberated on that date for a second.

"What happened on May 16th?" I questioned before I was quickly able to answer my own question. "That was the day of the murders. I don't understand. Why did your life end then?"

There was a part of me that felt grateful, but also guilty because I was supposed to have been there when the murders went down. If I hadn't got caught up showing my parents their new home, I would be dead too. Maybe Isaac was feeling that same guilt because he was supposed to be there too."

"Isaac, we were both lucky that circumstances kept us from being at that building when those murders happened. Don't feel like you beat death, it just wasn't our time. You can thank the man upstairs for that."

"No, it has nothing to do with the man upstairs," Isaac said sternly before then jumping right back into the uncontrollable sobs. "I would've never told him you were gonna be there if I knew they were gon' kill somebody. He said they were just gon' rob you... scare you a lil' bit," Isaac stuttered, rocking back and forth.

Now the room was spinning and I thought my head was about to explode. I refused to accept that I was hearing those words come out of Isaac's mouth. But now that he had begun his confession there was no putting a muzzle on

Isaac's mouth.

"Melanie told me she was pregnant and I knew it had to be mine, but she told me the baby she was carrying was yours. I had all this hatred towards you. Ever since we were little you always got everything and now you was gon' have the child that was supposed to be mine too."

"Isaac no," I kept repeating over and over again. "Tell me you not responsible for the murder of four innocent people because of the bullshit Melanie filled yo' head wit'. Man, please tell me that's not what you telling me."

"I wish I could," Isaac wailed. "I set you up to be robbed. So yes, it is my fault."

"That was the reason you reached out to me about the concert after you had been ignoring me for weeks?"

"Yes," he admitted, crying like a baby. "I started doing heroin right after that. The guilt, man. It was killin' me inside. I had to do something to numb the pain. I just wanted to die. I don't even deserve to live no more."

"Who did you give the information to?" In that split second, I went from wanting to do anything to get Isaac into rehab to willing to do anything to find out who the person was that set this shit in motion. Isaac continued with the nonstop tears and I was ready to punch the fuck out of him to shut up, but I needed answers. "Tell me who, Isaac!" I grabbed him firmly by the arms and wouldn't let him go. He was so thin I thought he was about to slip out my grasp.

"Arnez. I gave the information to Arnez." This nightmare didn't seem to have an end in sight. The information kept getting worse. I knew for sure that Isaac was going to name drop one of those robbing crews Sean had spoken about. Never did I believe it would be someone so close to home.

After Isaac's reveal, I let him go with the slightest of force. He was so flimsy his limp body flew down on the bed. "I'm so so sorry, X. I never wanted you to die. I never wanted anyone to die," he yowled. He sounded like a hit dog.

"Don't mention a word of what you told me to anyone, especially not Arnez. I'll give your mother the money to get you into the best rehab facility, but don't ever contact me again. We're done." I left out of Isaac's room sick to my stomach and there was only one thing that would take this ill sensation away.

Upon J-Rock's death, my level of fame had propelled quadruple. It was freakish in a way. I suppose it was a combination of all the media surrounding his death had in turn also put the spotlight on me. I was being introduced to a whole other audience of people who had never heard of Supreme and now they did. Then there were so many other people that simply sympathized with me and continued buying my music to show support. That somewhat bothered me because I was the last person that deserved any sympathy. The four people that were murdered in cold blood on that day were the only ones worthy of sympathy.

It had now been seven months since that fateful day and two weeks since the release of my album in memory of J-Rock. My second CD was on track to go multi platinum. I knew my mentor and friend was smiling down on me. I was on a fast track with my career seeming unstoppable. I was one of the biggest, if not the biggest, rapper in the world right now, but none of that weighed into the decision I had made.

For the last few months I sat on the information Isaac had revealed to me. I waited and plotted for the perfect time. As the case grew cold and police began shifting their attention to new cases I knew it was time for me to make my move. Like they always say, revenge is best served cold.

"Supreme, when you called and said you had a business proposition for me I was anxious to see what it was. Sit down. Can I get you something to drink?" Arnez offered as I sat down in his living room.

"No, I'm straight." For the last couple of months once I could stomach seeing Arnez's face and hearing his voice I began reaching back out to him as if everything was cool. I wanted to make sure he felt secure with the fact that his secret hadn't been exposed to me.

"Cool. Rob should be here any minute. He was glad you wanted to include him in this business venture," Arnez said pouring himself something to drink.

"It was only right. If it weren't for Rob I would've never met you. I thought this was a good way to show my appreciation."

"I agree." Arnez nodded. "That must be Rob now," he said when we heard the doorbell ring.

I sat quietly while Arnez let Rob in. I looked down at how white and clean the plush carpet was in the living room.

"What up, superstar!" Rob smiled, slapping my hand. "It's good to see you."

"Good to see you too, man." I smiled back before sitting back down. Rob then sat down on the couch across from me next to Arnez.

"Thanks for looking out for a brother and including me on whatever this new venture is. I know it's about some money since everyone in this room 'bout they paper," Rob boasted.

"I was telling Supreme the same thing. I always knew he was a good dude. You're once again proving me correct. You at the top of your game, but still looking out for the people that believed in you from the jump. Now that's showing love and loyalty," Arnez stated proudly.

I watched as Arnez and Rob got comfortable on the couch. They were completely oblivious at how much I loathed them. Both of these men had been a part of setting me up and killing my people in the process.

"So tell us, Supreme. What's our next move?" Rob wanted to know.

"How about one of you tell me why you had to kill J-Rock, Bailey, Davis, and Clint."

They both stared at me stone-faced, neither of them admitting to shit.

"Supreme, I don't know what you're talking about," Arnez said coolly shifting his body.

Rob was more abrupt with his approach. "I know you didn't have us meet to talk about some bullshit. Why the fuck is you wasting our motherfuckin' time!" Arnez was motioning to Rob to chill, but he was always a hothead. That's why I decided to go ahead and calm his ass down.

"I'ma need you to shut the fuck up and answer my question," I stated, pulling out my gun and aiming it directly at the two men. My finger was firmly gripped on the trigger so they understood this wasn't a game.

"Supreme, we're all friends here, put the gun away. There's no need for that," Arnez tried to reassure me.

"If I'm what you call a friend I hate to see what you do to your enemies."

"Nigga, stop acting like you a street nigga. Don't let that shit you rap about go to yo' motherfuckin' head," Rob growled.

"You right, I ain't no street nigga. I'm an intelligent gangster, which makes me ten times more deadly. But clearly you're a waste of my time, Rob, so fuck you," I said unloading two bullets directly to his head. I wanted to leave him without a face like they did to J-Rock. "I guess he won't be having an open casket."

The blood splatter had left its mark on the all-white décor including the plush carpet. Arnez wiped away some of the particles from Rob's brain that had splashed on his face with ease. He remained true to his composed demeanor even with a gun pointed to his head.

"Supreme, this has gotten way out of hand.

Rob is dead; you've proven your point. What can we do to end this unfortunate situation?"

"You can start by telling me why you had to kill them." Arnez's eyes darted around the room not wanting to give me any direct answers. "I really have no problem using this gun again," I said leaning forward.

"That won't be necessary. The truth of the matter is I carried around a grudge for you signing with J-Rock and never signing management papers with me."

"So when you came to my listening party saying all was forgiven that was all bullshit?" I asked with a raised eyebrow.

"Yes. You played me and I didn't like it. Rob warned me that would happen and I hated being wrong."

"So you sat back until you thought it was the right time to kill me?"

"That's where you have it wrong. It was never my intention to kill you. When I sent them to the office building I did expect you to be there, but they were to kill everyone in sight but let you live. It worked out perfectly that you weren't there anyway."

"That makes no sense, why did you want to let me live?"

"You're the moneymaker. Why would I want

the moneymaker to die?" Arnez chuckled like the shit was funny. "I figured after J-Rock was dead you would need someone to handle your business and who would be better for you to turn to than me. I was the one that gave you a real start. Even after you shitted on me, I made amends so I knew it was only a matter of time before you decided to give our business relationship another try."

"You had it all planned out… huh?"

"Pretty much and it would've worked if you hadn't found out the truth."

"The only reason why you're still alive is because I appreciate the fact that you did do a lot for me before my career took off. With that being said, this is the one and only lifeline I'm giving you."

"Thank you."

"Not so fast. This lifeline has stipulations. You have twenty-four hours to get out of New York. I don't care where you go, but it better be far, far away from here and take your business with you. If you're not gone in twenty-four hours you're a dead man. Don't try to make a move because I already have a hefty bounty over your head if you don't abide with my demands. Or if you prefer you can simply die now. Whatever works best for you."

"You continue to amaze me, Supreme. You

are a young man that wears many different faces and they're becoming more lethal."

"I'm not here to entertain you. What's it gonna be, Arnez?"

"I'll be gone first thing in the morning and I will be taking my business dealings with me. But trust me, Supreme, we'll be in touch again. You'll need me one day and I'll be more than happy to accommodate you."

"I'll leave you now. You have a lot of packing to do and some cleaning up," I said, glancing over at Rob's dead body.

While I drove away from Arnez's crib, that pain I thought would magically disappear once I got some form of justice, remained. My heart continued to ache and I reasoned that it would probably do so for the rest of my life. With time it might get easier, but the scars would forever linger.

Chapter Twelve

Who's That Girl

Five Years Later...

I sat across from the interviewer and after all these years of being in the business you would think this would all seem repetitive. Answering these questions about my career, how I got started, my greatest challenges and so on, but today was different. This was my first cover for

Rolling Stone Magazine. Yes, they had reached out to me for the cover a few years ago, but I was in a different place now.

"Supreme, this is your first album since the release of The Legacy Of J-Rock. That CD went on to sell over six million copies. How do you think your new album will do in comparison?'

"I make music for the people, my fans. I believe they will come out and support. I put my heart and soul into this CD and the music reflects it."

"You're with a new label now, Atomic Records. You've reportedly got one of the largest advances ever for an artist."

"So they say." I laughed. "But I'm not one to really discuss money, unless you owe me money of course. But seriously, Atomic is excellent and I feel honored to be a part of their company."

"Your first two CDs were released under your own label, Platinum Records, do you think being with a major will be beneficial or a hindrance?"

"Initially, I was skeptical about signing with a major. I didn't want my music to change or suffer because they wanted me to have a more mainstream sound. But after I sat down and had a few meetings with the bigwigs over there, they assured me that wasn't the case. I would still have creative control over my music, but also the huge budget to promote it on a larger scale. So I believe this will be a mutually beneficial relationship."

"I see. So what can fans expect from this CD?"

"Riley, I'ma need to answer that question in the car. I have an album release party to attend," I said, noticing my publicist waving her hand.

We left my hotel suite and hopped into the black Suburban parked out front. The driver made his way through the New York City streets until we pulled up to the venue on West 26th Street.

"I know we weren't able to do much talking on the ride over, but we'll be hanging out for the next few days, so you'll have plenty of time to get what you need."

"All this is good. This piece is about the artist and the person so just do what you do, Supreme, and I'm taking note.," Riley smiled. Something about Riley reminded me of Bailey. They didn't really look alike, but their carefree spirit was similar. After all these years, a day still didn't go by that I didn't think of him.

All that reminiscing quickly came to a halt once I exited the car and hit the red carpet. The glaring lights from the photographers and the ambush of media questions were standard and came with the job. I stood still for a couple minutes so the press could get their money shots then made my way inside.

"Wow! This is a great turn out," Riley commented, as we were lead to my VIP section.

"You're right. I wasn't expecting all of this," I replied as I shook hands and nodded my head acknowledging industry heavy weights and other artists who came through to show love. After being mostly out of the spotlight for the last few years it was a humbling experience to see so many people come out to support.

When we got to our table, the first person I noticed was Alisha. She stood up and gave me one of those fake industry kisses on the cheek, but I wouldn't expect anything less from her.

"I didn't think you were gonna make it," I said, sitting down next to her on the velvet couch.

"The photo shoot ended early. So I just took one of the dresses from the rack," she said caressing her hand down the curves of the lace nude and sheer dress she was wearing, "and headed here. Oh, this is Shar. She was the other model that was in the photo shoot with me."

I nodded my head towards Shar and she waved her hand while sipping on some champagne. She looked familiar to me, but I figured I had seen her in some magazine or television commercial. If she was working with Alisha then it was more than likely one or the other or maybe both.

"This party is everything. I've seen musicians, politicians, and of course actors and actresses. Do you actually know all these people?" Alisha questioned.

"Definitely not. But this is a party and most people aren't gonna turn down a good party."

"Well, the only reason I'm here is because of you," Alisha gushed, kissing me on the cheek. This time the kiss wasn't one of those fake Hollywood kisses. "I have a week off. I don't have to be in Paris until next weekend. We should get away. Between you working on your album and me traveling the world on this modeling shit we haven't had any quality time together in awhile. What do you say?"

"That sounds good. I have to do some promotional appearances for the album, but I'll be done with all that in a few days, then we can go away."

"You mean it?" Alisha questioned.

"I said it didn't I."

"You say a lot of things, but most of the time you change your mind. Is this gonna be one of them?"

"Nope, it's not," I said giving Alisha's exposed thigh an affectionate squeeze. She giggled before kissing me again, but this time on the lips.

Despite the Hollywood aura she would

sometimes put on, Alisha was a sweetheart and it was hard not to care about her. I first met her over six months ago when she was cast as the lead for the first single off of what was then my upcoming album. There was no denying she was drop dead gorgeous. She wasn't the typical tall skinny model. Yes, she had height on her, but also the curves to match. I had seen her in several high fashion magazines, but they did her no justice once I met her in person.

With all her beauty, sweetness, and success there was something lacking chemistry-wise. The sex was good, but it wasn't great. The conversation was cool, but not memorable. She was smart, but not witty. She could get my attention, but not keep it. But I was still willing to give it a try because out of all the women I had met, which were many, she was one of the few that were genuine and authentic. Alisha hadn't yet been completely turned out by the industry and I was drawn to that.

After about another hour of listening to music, having a couple of drinks, and idle chatter, I was ready to go. "Babe, I'm about to break out," I told Alisha while she was laughing and talking to her friend Shar.

"I can come with you," Alisha suggested, putting her drink down about to stand up.

"No, you stay here and keep your friend company. I have to finish this interview with Rolling Stone anyway," I said looking over at Riley. "Are you sure? I really don't mind." "I'm positive. Enjoy yourself. There's plenty of champagne and anything else you want. We're about to be permanently linked together for a few days anyway." "I'm looking forward to it." Alisha smiled. "Me too. I'll call you later on." I kissed Alisha goodbye and headed out.

My security, publicist, Riley and a few other people in my entourage followed me out to the Suburban. The press was still out front and also some paparazzi. My handlers were rushing me to the truck when I looked up and for a split second my eyes locked with a woman that I had never seen before. She had this captivating darkness to her eyes that pulled me in. Before I could utter a word, I was back in the Suburban being driven off.

Chapter Thirteen

Precious Cummings

"My man Supreme is up in the building!" the host announced over the live radio feed. "Your album has been number one for four consecutive weeks, how you feel about that? That's one hell of a comeback."

"The people still love me. That always feels good."

"We happy to have you here in Atlantic City."

"There's no place I would rather be. Funk Master Flex's annual car show is a classic event. I'm glad I could come and just be around my people." After chopping it up for a few more minutes with the host of the event I decided to walk around with my small entourage in tow. There were people coming up asking for autographs and photos, but for the most part it was chill. When I was signing one autograph I noticed a young lady that I thought I knew or maybe I just wanted to know. She had some nice fitted jeans and a plain white tank top, but there was nothing plain about her. The chick was bad. I stood studying her movements for a minute. I laughed to myself as she kept frowning at every nigga that was walking by trying to get her attention. The more I studied her the quicker it hit me. I began walking towards the mystery woman as my crew hurried behind me. As I got closer, her eyes met mine and she seemed unable to turn away.

"Didn't I see you outside a club about a month ago?" I asked her. She seemed distracted looking at some of my boys and a couple of bodyguards lingering beside me.

"Aren't you the rapper, Supreme?"

"Yeah, that's me," I replied in a mellow tone.

"Aren't you the young lady that was going

into the club as I was leaving?"

"Yeah, that was me. You remember that." By the way she asked the question I could tell she was surprised.

"Of course, I'd never forget a face as beautiful as yours."

"Why you tryna make me blush in front of all these people out here?"

"That wasn't my intention. What I wanted was for you to walk with me, talk with me and then, hopefully exchange numbers with me. But that might be asking too much. What do you think?"

"Truthfully, I want to leave with you, be with you, and hopefully chill with you for a long time."

I was digging her comeback, but before I could give my response a girl I knew walked up.

"What's up, Supreme?" Rhonda said giving me a hug.

"Just so you know. I work with her... that's it," I explained not wanting her to feel uncomfortable.

"Supreme, that's my roommate. You don't have to explain yourself."

"Word. You guys live together? Damn, Rhonda you never told me you had this at home." I pointed at my crush like she was this perfectly wrapped gift exclusively made for me.

"She came to your album release party, but I

think you had already left."

"Yeah, we made eye contact on my way out. Then I was blessed to see her once again today. Damn, baby, I didn't even get your name yet."

"Precious."

"That name fits you perfectly. So are you going to walk with me or what?"

"That depends. Are you going to leave with me, be with me, and chill with me?"

"You didn't even have to ask me that twice. I heard you the first time and the answer is no doubt."

With that, I took Precious's hand and spent the entire duration of the car show with her as my date. Later on that night we had dinner and drinks with my entire crew and Rhonda came too. I had never laughed this much with a female in my life. I instantly clicked with her. We fit without it feeling forced at all.

"So are you leaving with Rhonda or are you staying with me?" I whispered in Precious's ear while she finished the last of her drink.

"That's a silly question. I'm going with you. Oh, you didn't know... you ain't gon' ever be able to get rid of me."

Some might think a woman saying that to me would scare off a man in my position, but it was the exact opposite. I wanted Precious even more because I never wanted to get rid of her either.

"Do you mind if I take a shower?" Precious asked when we got back to my hotel suite at the Borgata.

"Of course. Make yourself comfortable."

"Thanks. I won't be gone that long." While Precious was taking a shower, I turned on the television and lay down on the bed. Before I could get comfortable I noticed Alisha was calling me. My initial reaction was to answer since that is what I would typically do, but who knew in just a few short hours my love life had changed.

"Are you gonna get that?" I glanced up and Precious was standing in the doorway of the bathroom naked. Her body was glistening from the water still on her body.

"No, I'm straight."

Precious slid in the bed next to me and began kissing my chest as her tongue was making its way down. Before she could go any further I stopped her. "Precious, I just want you to fall asleep in my arms."

"I can do that right after we fuck."

"Baby, I don't want to fuck you."

"What you mean you don't want to fuck me? What is something wrong wit' me or something?" This gaze came over her face like she was embarrassed and that was never my intention.

"Precious, look at me," I said, grabbing her face. "Physically, you're perfect. And I want you in every way. When we become intimate, I don't want us to fuck. I want us to make love. There is a big difference. Precious, I'm truly feeling you. I was connected to you in just that brief moment we locked eyes in front of the club.

"You're special and I want our relationship to be special. That means taking our time and getting to know one another; getting past the lust and learning to appreciate what's on the inside. Will you do that with me, Precious? Take our time so we can build something real?"

I don't know if it was because Precious was taken aback by what I said or she had no idea how to respond. But instead of giving me any sort of reply she snuggled her naked body underneath my arms and fell asleep.

Chapter Fourteen

Is That Your Girlfriend

For the next few weeks I spent all my available time with Precious. If I wasn't in the studio or preparing for my show tonight at the Garden then I was with her, if I wasn't taking meetings I was with her. I wanted to know everything I could about this woman and the more time we spent together the more intrigued I became. On my way to the in-store promo signing I was doing at a record store in Manhattan, I was wishing she were sitting next to me in the car. So when I heard my cell, I didn't even bother to see who was calling because my mind was on her. I didn't even say anything when I first answered that's how far done my mind was.

"Hello... hello... Supreme is that you?"

Hearing Alisha's voice brought me back current. "Alisha, hey how are you?"

"That's all you got for me? I've been calling you. Left you a ton of messages and all you got for me is a 'hey, how are you.' I'm not fuckin' good, Supreme."

"I'm sorry to hear that. I apologize for not getting back to you. I've been in the studio a lot. I haven't had any free time," I lied which I hated doing because Alisha was a cool chick.

"Oh really, you haven't had any free time? So who was the girl you were having dinner with last night?"

"Huh?" I knew how dumb I sounded right after I said it, but Alisha's question threw me for a loop. I wasn't expecting that to come out of her mouth.

"Don't huh me. My girlfriend Shar saw you at the restaurant in the Four Seasons Hotel last night. She saw you kissing and holding hands with that chick. Who is she, Supreme, and don't lie and say she's just a friend. You are not taking a friend to the fuckin' Four Seasons," Alisha screamed in the phone.

I had never heard Alisha yell before, but I guess because I had never given her a reason. I felt horrible that she had to find out about Precious like this, but I had no one to blame but myself. I should've come clean the second I knew that Precious was the one for me which was since the first day we met.

"Alisha, I'm about to walk into this store for this promo I'm doing. I'ma call you as soon as I leave. I have my concert tonight, but maybe I can come over tomorrow so we can talk. I don't want things to end on some negative shit."

"I think you've said everything I need to hear. I guess you knew a long time ago things had ended between us. Thanks for finally letting me know!"

"Alisha wait!" I called out, but she had already hung up. I felt like shit. Alisha had been the closest thing to a girlfriend I ever had and to hear how hurt she was made me feel horrible. Alisha didn't deserve that, but I had no clue how to make it right.

"Sir, they're waiting for you," I heard the driver say, snapping me out of my thoughts. There were like four people waiting outside the car door. Then my security was in the car behind me because I wanted to ride alone. Sometimes I got like that, just wanting some privacy... alone time.

When I got out the car, I was stupefied to see the line wrapped around the building. They actually had to shut the street down because it reached to the very end of the block. After all this time, I never stopped being amazed that all these people would show up just to meet me... Xavier Mills from Queens.

Once inside, shit was moving mad fast. They were rushing people in and out due to the huge turnout. I was doing my best to give fans as much attention as I could so they would feel like I was worth the wait. The last thing I wanted was for them to feel like standing on their feet for hours was a waste of their time.

When the next CD was placed on the table in front of me I was so busy trying to sign it and not interrupt the momentum that at first I didn't look up. "What's your name?" I questioned so I could personalize the autograph.

"Isaac. My name is Isaac." The name and familiar voice made me pause and glance up. My mouth dropped. My childhood best friend who I hadn't seen in what felt like a lifetime was standing in front of me. "Look at you, man. All these people here for you. You did good. I'm so proud of you, X."

"Sir, you need to take your CD and move on," one of my handlers directed Isaac.

"Hold up," I said standing up. "Give me a moment." The handler moved back and it was then that I noticed a little boy who looked no more than five holding Isaac's hand. "Wow, what a handsome young man. He looks like you spit him out." The little boy smiled and that shit really warmed my heart.

"This is Jalen, my son," Isaac said proudly.

"Ain't no denying that." We laughed. "He looks just like you. It's scary. Looking at him makes me feel like I'm five again."

"Yeah, he's been a real blessing to me. He's the reason I got my life together," Isaac disclosed.

"I'm glad to hear that. You look really good. You married?" I questioned noticing the wedding band.

"Yes. Melanie and I got married. After she had Jalen, she really helped me get my life together. We've both done a lot of growing up."

"I'm happy for you, Isaac. I really am."

"I know you might never forgive me for what happened, but I had to see you and let you know how sorry I am. I also wanted you to meet my son. How ironic that he turned out to be mine after all."

"God makes no mistakes."

"He sure doesn't. I'm not going to hold you up any longer. These people gonna kill me in a minute if I don't get out the way. It was really good seeing you, X."

"It was really good seeing you, too," I said giving Isaac a hug and his son a hug too. "You take care of yourself and your beautiful son. Until next time."

Part of me wanted to pull Isaac back in my life, but instead I let him walk away. He was my brother and would always be, but the cut was way too deep. I didn't think either of us would ever completely heal from what happened five years ago. We both carried guilt, but for different reasons. I do believe seeing each other this one last time gave us the closure that we needed to at least find peace and move on.

This night brought back so many memories for me. It was just over five years ago I was supposed to be opening up for J-Rock at Madison Square Garden, but that show was cancelled because he was murdered. Now, after all this time, the concert that never happened, finally did. But I didn't open the show, I closed it. It was bittersweet in a lot of ways. I knew J-Rock and Bailey were smiling down on me when I stood on stage in front of a sold-out crowd and spit hit after hit after hit.

Only one thing was missing or better yet one person, Precious. I had given her a ticket and a backstage pass, but she was a no-show. She wasn't answering her phone and after waiting for a while I went ahead and headed to my after party at the W Hotel. When I got to the penthouse suite, it was already wall-to-wall packed. I weaved through the massive crowd until I got to a back area that had a private sitting spot so I didn't have to be so up under everybody. I had two of my security guards with me so they were able to quickly get me through the throngs of people without much hassle.

I wasn't seated for more than five minutes when Alisha approached. My security was very familiar with her so they let her right through. I wasn't sure what she had to say, but I knew it wasn't good.

"I'm sure I'm the last person you were expecting to see," Alisha said, sitting down.

"After the way you hung up on me earlier, I have to say this is a surprise."

"I was beyond angry with you and I swore I would never speak to you again. I even deleted your number from my phone, but I—"

"Alisha, I'm so sorry. I never—"

"Just let me finish," she said, cutting me off. "I battled with myself the entire time I was on my way over here because I felt so stupid."

"You have no reason to feel stupid. I'm the one that fucked up not you."

"When you say you're the one that fucked up it sounds like you're saying you made a mistake. Does that mean you regret whatever you had going on with that other girl and you want to give us another try?"

Alisha had these perfect full lips and when she was speaking to me, I thought about how those perfect lips looked while wrapped around my dick when she gave me head. She didn't give me amazing head, but she always looked damn near perfect while doing it. So when Alisha asked me did I want to give us another try, I was almost tempted to say yes, but I knew it would be wrong and she didn't deserve that.

"Alisha, you know I care about you."

"I thought you did. I know we both have super busy schedules, but we seemed to be making time for each other and trying to make it work. Then all of a sudden a couple months ago you became distant overnight. After I was supposed to attend that car show with you, but at the last minute I had to fly to LA for a photo shoot that I couldn't get out of, you seemed to just cut me off. Is that what triggered you to start seeing someone else?"

I let out a deep sigh because I wasn't sure how to answer Alisha's question. I wanted to be honest with her, but not so honest that I crushed her feelings. "I did meet somebody, Alisha."

"You're talking about the girl Shar saw you at the restaurant with?"

"Yes and things are getting serious between us."

"How long have you been seeing her... were you seeing her while we were supposed to be together because I thought we were pretty exclusive. I mean, I was exclusive to you," Alisha said with sadness in her voice. "I guess it was one-sided."

"That's not true. I wasn't seeing anyone else when we were together."

"Then when did you have time to get serious with this new girl you're seeing?"

"I met her at the car show," I admitted. "We just clicked."

"Wow. I wasn't able to go to the car show with you and lost my man to another woman in the process," Alisha sulked, shaking her head.

"Don't look at it like that. It wasn't planned sometimes things just happen. That doesn't change how I feel about you and the time we spent together."

"You don't have to say anymore, Supreme. I got all the answers I needed and at least I got some closure so I'm glad I came."

"I'm glad you came too. You're special, Alisha. I always told you that and it's true."

"Thank you, but let me get out of here before I start embarrassing myself. I really hope this new girl in your life treats you right because we could've been great together. Take care, Supreme." Alisha gave me a goodbye kiss and her lips were still soft as ever. She strutted away with poise and grace like she was working the runway. As perfect as she was in so many ways, she just wasn't Precious.

Once Alisha left, I knocked back a few drinks to take the edge off. This was supposed to be a party, but having that deep ass conversation with her put me in a dark mood, which was defeating the purpose of celebrating. It didn't take long for the liquor to kick in and I started talking with people and enjoying myself.

"Oh, so I guess you found someone to keep you company, huh, Supreme?" I had to do a double take for a second because I was completely caught off guard. But I quickly regrouped once I put the face and the voice together.

"Precious, I'm glad you made it. I waited for you backstage, but you never came."

"So what, you scooped up the first piece of ass you could to replace me?"

"Excuse me?" the girl sitting next to me looked at Precious and said.

"Bitch, you heard what the fuck I said. Why don't you sit there like the good mutt you are and mind yo' business. This here is between me and Supreme."

"Listen, I don't know who you think you are, but—" before the girl could continue, I tried to defuse the situation.

"I apologize," I said to the young lady. "Precious is a very close friend of mine, and she is misreading what's going on between us, which, for the record, is nothing," I added, turning to look at Precious to make sure she understood she was getting pissed off for no fuckin' reason.

"Fuck you, Supreme. I knew you were full of shit. Is that why you don't fuck me, 'cause you like putting your dick in bitches like her? You stay here and entertain your little friend. I'm out."

Before I could counter, Precious bolted through the crowd like she was furious. I rushed to catch up to her, but she was moving with such swiftness I was barely able to keep up. Finally getting through the jungle of people, when I reached the hallway my eyes zoomed in on my target and it wasn't a pleasant sight to see. Precious was leaned up against the wall with some nigga's tongue down her throat. *Fuck this* were the words that initially popped up in my head. My body began the motion of turning around and leaving Precious right where she was, up against that wall. But then I stopped. I knew she was reacting out of anger and I wasn't ready to wipe my hands of her because of that.

"What the fuck is you doing!" I barked, yanking her arms from around the dude she was posted up with against the wall.

"Supreme, yo' this your girl?" the guy questioned in a fearful tone like he didn't want no problems.

"No, I'm just his close friend," Precious snapped back with sarcasm.

"Yeah, this my girl."

"That's not what you called me when you were getting all cozy wit' miss Jenny from the block."

"Yo, shut the fuck up." I shook my head mad that Precious had gotten me so riled up.

"Man, I'm sorry. I didn't know that was your girl."

Somebody must've told my bodyguards there was some sort of altercation going on, because all of a sudden they came out ready to take down the dude Precious had been kissing on. "Everything's cool," I made clear wanting to bring the unnecessary commotion to an end. "But, you can go now," I informed the guy, wanting him away from Precious and me. I then grabbed her arm until we got to a door at the other end of the hall.

I took out my key, opened the door, and pulled her into another suite. "What the fuck is wrong with you, Precious?" I roared after slamming the door closed.

"What the fuck is wrong wit' me? What about you. Carrying on wit' that bitch."

"We were talking, that's it. If you had gotten to the show on time and met me backstage like you were supposed to, then I wouldn't have to talk to nobody else."

"Oh, so now it's my fault you kicking it wit' the next bitch. I guess it's my fault, too, that you don't want to have sex wit' me."

"Is that with this is about? You want me to fuck you, is that what you want, Precious? Hum, answer me." I was now grabbing her roughly, pulling on her dress. I put my hands around her waist and forcefully pushed her hips towards me. "Oh, now you don't have nothing to say. Either you want me to fuck you or you don't, Precious.

Which one is it?"

Precious remained silent, but yet she wasn't turning me away so I took it up a notch. I put my hands up her dress and ripped off her thong.

"How do you want me to fuck you, Precious, from the front or the back?" She still wasn't saying a word, but the moans she was making that sounded like a woman in heat let me know I was giving her exactly what she wanted. I flipped her body around and bent Precious over a chair. She was so wet, that my hardened dick slid inside of her with ease. With each thrust her pussy seemed to be singing my name.

"Oh, Supreme, baby you feel so good," she moaned. It felt so right being inside of her, but on the flipside I was pissed for the bullshit she pulled.

"You was going to give all this ass to some nigga you didn't even know."

"No, baby, I was just tryna make you jealous."

"Don't lie to me."

"I swear, I only want you."

"You better 'cause this pussy is mine now. If you ever try some trifling shit like that again, I will fuck you up. You understand me?"

"Yes."

"You sure?"

"Yes, it won't neva happen again."

In my mind when I envisioned our first time, I romanticized it as us making love. It wasn't like this. It wasn't full of anger mixed with lust and passion. But Precious was such a fireball, I shouldn't have expected anything less.

Chapter Fifteen

Say I Do

"I can't believe I'm about to meet your parents." Precious sighed nervously, squeezing my hand as I drove to their house.

"Now that we're engaged I think it's time." I glanced over and smiled at Precious reassuringly before putting my eyes back on the road.

Over the last several months, Precious and I had our ups and downs. At one point I wasn't sure we were gonna make it. I knew she loved me, but I also knew she had a lot of shit wit' her that she didn't want to share. I understood we all had secrets, hell I had a few of my own, but I had zero tolerance for games. But after a few bumps in the road, Precious finally came clean to me about her past and the people that had been in her life, including her ex-boyfriend, Nico Carter, who was serving life in prison. Her opening up and telling me the truth only made us closer and our bond even stronger. It also solidified to me that she was the woman I wanted to spend the rest of my life with, so I had to put a ring on it and make her my wife. Now it was only right that I introduced her to the two most important people in my life other than her.

"What a beautiful house," Precious commented when we pulled up in the circular driveway.

"I actually recently bought them this house. I thought it was time for an upgrade from the previous house I bought them."

"Gosh, I bet your parents love you. Most kids aren't able and the ones that are still wouldn't buy their parents a home like this," Precious said in awe of the private gated home.

I had to admit that house was nice. It was an elegant palatial resort-style home with tennis court, pool, gym, theater, beauty salon, elevator and serving kitchen. The crazy part was the house was originally supposed to be for me, but I decided to pass on it and buy it for my parents instead. My mother didn't truly believe this was their new home until I had all their clothes and belongings packed up and moved to the new crib. She's been on cloud nine ever since.

"Do you think I look okay?" Precious questioned when we got out the car and was walking towards the entrance.

"You look amazing like you always do," I said admiring the pale pink wrap dress she had on with open toe heels. Her hair was slicked back in a loose ponytail and her makeup was subtle, but she was wearing some lip-gloss that matched her dress perfectly.

"Thanks." Precious blushed. "You always know exactly what to say to make me feel loved."

"That's because you are loved." I kissed her on the length of her slim neck right before I rung the doorbell.

"Baby, you made it!" My mom beamed when she answered the door to let us in.

"I told you I was coming." I smiled giving her a hug. "Mom, this is my fiancé Precious."

"It is such a pleasure to meet you, Precious. Your dress is very pretty and you're just as beautiful as my son described. And my goodness look at that ring... it is breathtaking."

"Thank you and it's such a pleasure to meet you too." The two of them hugged and everything felt right.

"Follow me," my mom said after releasing Precious from her embrace. "I just took the food out the oven so dinner is ready to be served."

As we followed my mom to the dining room, Precious was squeezing my hand tightly. I had never seen her so nervous before, but I found it to be so cute. I tried to tell her not to worry that all would go good, but I guess I wasn't convincing enough.

After introducing my dad and Precious, the four of us sat down at the table and dinner was served. My dad told a few of his less than funny jokes that we all graciously laughed at. Then my mom asked me a few questions regarding what I was currently working on before she then turned the conversation to Precious.

"Supreme has spoken very highly of you, Precious," my mom informed her.

"Yes, he has." My dad nodded between bites of his macaroni and cheese.

"I'm glad to hear that. Supreme is amazing," she turned to me and said.

"So are you," I said squeezing her hand.

"I know this engagement happened rather fast so have your parents had a chance to meet Supreme yet?" my mom asked.

"My mom actually died a couple years ago."

"We're so sorry to hear that," my parents said.

"What about your father?" my dad questioned.

"I... I never met my father before," Precious revealed, putting her head down.

"But that's okay, because she has me." I wanted Precious to be confident in my love for her and not feel ashamed about her family dynamics.

"So what do you do for a living, young lady?" of course my father had to ask.

"I'm actually between jobs right now. I'm considering going to school."

"To study what?" he said not letting up.

"I haven't decided yet." Precious laughed with uncertainty.

"She has time to figure it out. Right now we have a wedding to plan. Isn't that right, babe." I gave her a warm smile.

"Yes, and I can't wait."

"I'm sure you can't," I heard my mother mumble under her breath. I don't think Precious caught it, but I did.

"Mom, the last time I was over here I think I left something in the library. Can you come with me while I go check and see."

"Sure."

"Dad, make sure you don't go overboard with the entertainment while we're gone," I joked. "I'll be back shortly," I told Precious, kissing her on the cheek. By the time I did that my mother had already disappeared to the office.

"So what did you leave in here?" my mother questioned when I closed the door.

"Mom, you know I didn't leave anything. I wanted to speak to you in private."

My mother tried to give me this look like she didn't know what I was talking about. "Supreme, I'm confused. What did you need to speak to me about in private?"

"I heard what you said in there. Luckily, I don't think Precious did." She huffed as if irritated for me calling her out, but I didn't care. "Mom, Precious is going to be my wife and—"

"Well, she isn't your wife yet," my mother interjected before I could finish my sentence.

"What is that supposed to mean?"

"Are you sure this is the type of woman you want to marry? She has no job, no parents, no nothing, just you. It's almost like she was hatched and then left to fend for herself."

"That was her life before me. Precious has always had to take care of herself. She never had anyone to rely on. The odds were not stacked in her favor, but she overcame all of that."

"I get it. You see her as some sort of underdog. Kinda like you saw yourself when you were struggling to become a rapper. But, baby, you had real talent. You were also always very smart and driven. I've met young ladies like Precious before and the only thing that drives them is money and they think a cute face and a small waist will get it for them. That's their only ambition in life. But you've been in this entertainment industry for many years now. I would think it would take much more than that for a woman to lock you down. She ain't pregnant is she?" My mom frowned up her face and folded her arms like she had figured out some great mystery.

"No, Precious isn't pregnant. Even if she was, that's not the reason I'm marrying her."

"Then what is it? What makes her so much more special then all the other gorgeous women you've come across because I can't see anything else she's bringing to the table besides her looks. And, baby, let me tell you, them looks are the first thing that fades when you figure out somebody shady. They turn uglier than a motherfucker."

Growing up I always loved how real my mother kept it. She wasn't gonna sugarcoat shit.

So I knew where she was coming from when it came to Precious, but that didn't mean I was trying to hear it.

"I'm going to keep it one hundred with you, Mom. I can't pinpoint what makes her so much more special than the others, but that's the reason I know she's the one. The others never made me want to wake up each day with them lying by my side. The others never made me imagine how unfulfilled my life would be if they weren't in it."

"That's a beautiful thing, son, but it doesn't mean you have to marry her. What's the rush? You're so young and so successful. There are a ton of beautiful, successful, smart women out there that you haven't even met yet. Give yourself some time."

"I don't need time. I found the woman that I want to spend the rest of my life with. From the day I met her I knew in my heart she was the only woman for me. Don't get me wrong, I know Precious comes with a lot of baggage. Before I proposed she was very open with me about her past, but you know what, I still put a ring on her finger. The reason is because I love her, flaws and all."

"You know you will always be my baby, but I also know you are a grown man and I respect your decision. I will always be in your corner and support whatever decision you make whether I agree with it or not."

"That means so much to me. You know how much I love you and it's important to me that the two of you get along."

"Supreme, you don't ever have to worry about that. If that's the woman you choose to take as your wife then she's my family too. I will love that girl like she's my daughter because that's how much I love you."

"How did I get so lucky to have a mom like you?"

"Thank you, boo, but all my friends be asking me how did I get so lucky to have a son like you. I guess we both lucky." My mom beamed before wrapping her warm arms around me as we stood in the middle of the room holding each other tightly.

Within the next five months Precious and I had our elaborate summer wedding on the six-acre estate I purchased for us and she was pregnant with our first child. My life now superseded every dream I envisioned for myself. I was now floating on this ultimate high. It was reminiscent of that high when I was signed to Platinum Records and had the number one single and CD simultaneously. But like any high, you eventually come crashing down and for me that was when I walked into the bloodbath discovering J-Rock's and Bailey's dead bodies. So what was about to happen next should've came as no surprise to me as it seemed to be my destiny.

After the driver pulled through the iron gates, and we got closer to the estate, I could see Precious standing near her car in the front entrance of the house and a man pointing a gun directly at her. At that second I would've given anything to be able to switch places with her. Not only was she my wife, but she was also the mother of my unborn child.

"Hurry the fuck up!" I roared at the driver, but he wasn't moving fast enough for me so I jumped out. As I hauled ass towards toward them, I saw Precious and the shooter both glance in my direction. Even from the distance, I could see the fear in Precious's eyes. I heard my bodyguards racing behind me. I knew they were strapped, but it was too late. When what sounded like an explosion ripped through air, it felt like the bullet struck me. That's how much pain my heart was in.

The shooter then began spraying bullets in our direction. The way he quickly vanished into the darkness, I knew the gunfire was more so to shield himself as he made his getaway. My bodyguards continued firing shots trying to take the gunman down, but to no avail.

I saw Precious's body jolt back falling down on the ground. When I reached her, she was lying in a pool of blood barely holding on. She looked so weak as I cradled her limp body.

"Precious, baby, it's me, Supreme. Please stay with me. The ambulance will be here any minute. Baby, please, just hold on."

"Supreme, I'm so happy I was able to see your face one last time. Baby, I love you. I never knew what love was until I found you. Please forgive me for leaving you and taking our baby too."

"Dear God, with everything inside me, I'm begging you, please don't take Precious away from me. My life isn't even worth living if I don't have her in it."

Precious was struggling to stay alive as her strength quickly deteriorated and the blood continued to flow. She seemed to be battling between staying here with me or letting go, so her body could be at peace. I held onto her tightly because I knew if I let her go she would die right now in my arms. When her eyelids finally closed, I pulled Precious's body to my chest while I unleashed every tear inside of me.

Chapter Sixteen

A Dead Man Can't Talk

By the Grace Of God, Precious survived being shot by her ex-man, Nico Carter. When I realized it was him that pulled the trigger, I hired the best private investigators that money could buy to hunt him down like the animal he was and take him out. I refused to rely solely on the police to retrieve him from whatever gutter he had crawled into. I wouldn't be able to get one peaceful night's sleep until revenge was mine. The only saving grace in this tragedy was that even though our unborn child didn't survive, Precious did.

I never left Precious as she recuperated in the hospital from the emergency surgery performed to save her life. It took over four weeks, but she was finally given clearance to come home.

"I can't believe I'm finally getting out of this place." Precious smiled as I pushed her down the hallway in the wheelchair the nurse gave me. Precious wanted to leave it at the door, but it was mandatory hospital policy.

"I know. You're going home where you belong. I made sure everything was prepared for your arrival including implementing extra security. I guarantee you that Nico Carter will never harm you again." I kissed Precious on her forehead. She had been through so much and I knew she was mourning the loss of our child. It was imperative to me that I make her feel safe and protected.

"I love you so much, Supreme. I wouldn't be able to make it through this without you. You're my rock, baby." Precious squeezed my hand as the automatic doors opened and I wheeled her through.

"You don't have to worry about that, 'cause I'm never leaving your side," I reassured her as we made our way outside.

"Wow, it's so beautiful out. There's nothing like a warm, beautiful, sunny day to make everything in the world seem alright, if only for a moment." Even at this sad time, Precious was trying to stay positive. I loved and respected her even more for that.

When Precious noticed the Suburban parked right out front with my bodyguards posted beside it, she hopped out of the wheelchair quickly.

"Slow down, babe. You just got out the hospital. I don't want you going back," I joked.

"I'm fine... I'm better than fine. So much better that I'm tempted to run towards the truck."

"Please don't do that." I laughed, pushing the wheelchair off to the side. When I focused my attention back on Precious, I saw that something had caught her eye. When I glanced in the direction that had her transfixed, I could see a black van slowly approaching with its window rolled down. Before I could lock gazes with the passenger, the ringing of a machine gun spraying bullets filled the hot summer air.

"Precious, get down!" I barked throwing my body on top of hers to shield her from the gunfire. I could hear screams of innocent bystanders as the shooter kept firing not caring what other lives were lost in the process. When the shots finally ceased, I instinctively wanted to stand up and make sure Precious was okay. My mind was moving, but my body remained still. It was the most bizarre shit until I realized several of those bullets had penetrated me. Voices and sounds began fading away until I couldn't hear a damn thing, not even the sound of my own voice.

When I opened my eyes for a millisecond I thought I was back in the hospital room with Precious. But with the tubes and IVs attached to my body it was obvious that this time I was the patient. I tried to lift myself up off the bed, but that was a bad idea. "Oh shiiiiit!" I moaned as this excruciating pain shot through my body.

"I'll go get the nurse," I heard a man say.

"And bring the doctor, too," I howled.

When the nurse came in, the first thing she did was give me some pain medicine and I loved her for that.

"Mr. Mills, give it a few minutes, but the medicine will kick in shortly," she informed me.

"What hospital am I at and where is my

wife?" I questioned, feeling like something was off.

"I'll let them tell you," the nurse said, nodding her head to the right before checking my vital signs. After she was done and left the room two men stood up and approached the bed.

"I'm Agent McCoy, this is Agent Chimes and we're with the FBI."

"Okay... so what does the FBI want with me?"

"Do you remember what happened to you, Mr. Mills?" Agent McCoy asked.

"I remember being shot outside the hospital when I was leaving with my wife. I didn't get to see his face, but I believe Nico Carter is the one who did it. He already tried to kill my wife once. I guess he came back hoping to get it right the second time."

"Actually, Mr. Carter, is still on the run. He wasn't the one responsible for shooting you," the agent informed me.

"If it wasn't Nico, then who?"

"Michael Owens, also goes by Pretty Boy Mike. That is the person we believe is responsible for the shooting."

"That motherfucker. Well, have you arrested his ass?"

"Not yet."

"Why the hell not?"

"We've been building a case against Mr. Owens for a very long time. There is a laundry list of crimes, but to name a few, drug trafficking, money laundering, and now attempted murder. But we're still gathering evidence, as we want to make sure we can make the indictment stick. In the meantime, we want to keep you in protective custody."

"Protective custody?!" I wasn't feeling none of that.

"Yes. It's for your own protection. It's better for Mr. Owens to believe you're dead until we get all the evidence we need to send him away to prison for the rest of his life," Agent Chimes tried to convince me.

"So how long do you all need to get this done and why does Mike want me dead?"

"We're not sure, but this case is a top priority and so is saving your life. As to the reason Mr. Owens wants you dead, it's complicated. We can't give you all the details yet, but once we have a solid case, you'll never have to worry about Mike Owens again."

"Okay, so when can I see my family?" The two agents glanced at each other and then back at me. Neither one of them wanted to speak up after running off at the mouth nonstop a minute ago.

"No one including your family can know you're alive until after we've issued an arrest warrant for Mr. Owens and he is in our custody," Agent McCoy finally mustered up enough balls to say.

"You cannot be fuckin' serious!"

"I understand this is an inconvenience, but you almost died and we want you to stay alive."

"What about my wife? Is she in danger?"

"From all indications, Mr. Owens has no interest in harming your wife. You were the intended target. We do have assigned agents keeping an eye on her so she will be protected."

"She better be because if Mike does anything to my wife, I'm holding you all responsible."

"That's why we need for you to cooperate. The quicker we bring down Mr. Owens, the sooner you can get back home to your wife."

The last sentence is what got me through the next several months. After making a full recovery in a private hospital, I was then moved to a safe house on Long Island where I spent the remainder of my time while the world believed I was dead. The Feds kept me completely isolated so that the television and the multiple agents assigned to me became my only outlet into the real world.

It got to the point that I was telling them to turn off the television or keep that shit on mute because I was tired and disgusted with the media coverage of my so-called death. I had lost count of all the times I was ready to bolt out the door and see my family. But I understood the importance of making sure Mike's punk ass was locked up first. Not only for my safety, but also for my family's. Precious had been through enough and when we were able to reunite, I prayed that not only would Mike be out of our lives forever, but so would Nico. Until that happened, I had to continue to be a part of whatever game the Feds left me no choice but to play.

Chapter Seventeen

Love For Life

I kept replaying the disbelief that consumed Precious's face when I basically rose from the dead right before her eyes, as I watched her sleep. Last night, the only words she could muster up to say was, "Supreme, is that really you?"

After her ordeal with Mike, Precious was now resting peacefully. Being able to be by her side and watch her sleep after all these months put my entire life into perspective.

"How long have you been up?" she questioned, waking up from a deep sleep.

"Since you fell asleep last night. All this time being away from you I dreamed of just watching you sleep. These last few months have been the hardest of my life."

"Tell me what happened. I need to know the truth."

I stood up from the chair and sat down at the edge of the bed. Precious then sat up as if wanting me to know she was giving me her full attention. I took a deep breath and began telling her what my life had been like since I had been gone. I was eager to share my story.

"After you got shot and was in the hospital, Mike came to me offering a deal to sign with his record label. Of course I turned him down. He reached out to me a few more times afterwards, and I knew he was furious, but never did I believe he would resort to murder.

When I was shot leaving the hospital with you, the doctors performed emergency surgery, and I was in critical condition, but they knew I would survive. They told you and everyone else I had died, following the orders of the police and the FBI."

"But why?"

"Because the FBI had been trying to build a

case against Mike on drugs, money laundering, and all sorts of other crimes for a minute. They had an informant in place that had got word that Mike was responsible for the hit on me, but the FBI needed more proof. They wanted Mike to believe that I was dead to protect me until they had all the evidence needed to get an indictment and conviction."

"But... but I saw you die."

"So you thought. But after they took me in for emergency surgery, what followed was all staged. Baby, you have no idea what the government can do. After they declared me dead and took me into hiding, the Feds transferred me to one of their hospitals, where they nursed me back to health. Having you and my parents grieving over me and watching mad people mourn my death when I was very much alive, that shit was hard. Harder than being shot seven times.

"Precious, I was watching the whole thing on TV from my bed. Even when you were crying over my casket, you looked beautiful. I wanted to reach through the television and hold you so you would know everything would be okay because I was alive. After my ordeal, I'm starting to question whether those Tupac rumors are true," I said, wondering that shit foreal.

"So where were you for all these months?"

"In a safe house somewhere on Long Island. They had me stashed under lock and key. They kept me in the dark about how the investigation was going. A few police officers were with me 24/7 for protection, but they wouldn't tell me shit. Luckily, I overheard one of them talking about the cops making their move on Mike, because they believed you were in imminent danger. I told them if they didn't take me to you I would go on my own, and the only way to stop me was to kill me. They could see I was dead-ass serious, so they took me to you.

"I was stressing the whole time because I didn't know what the fuck was going on. All I knew was that you were with Mike. Baby, I'm so sorry I couldn't protect you from that piece of shit. I wanted to kill that nigga with my bare hands." I was ready to explode just thinking about what Mike did to Precious but I knew with everything she had been through, my wife needed me to keep my anger in check.

"I still can't believe you're alive. Since you've been gone my life has been on a downward spiral. I never thought I would touch you or hold you again. Or feel you make love to me. The only reason I wanted to live was to revenge your death." Precious was trying to remain strong but I could see the pain and disbelief in her eyes.

"I know how hard it's been for you, baby. But I'm here, and starting right now we're making up for our lost time."

"Can we start by you making love to me?"

"Are you sure you're ready for that? After what happened with Mike, I understand if you need time and want to wait." With the sweetness in her face it was hard for me to deny her and honestly I didn't want to.

"I want to forget about Mike and what he did to me. Today is a new beginning, and I want to share it with you. I need to feel you inside of me, so I'll know you'll never leave me again."

"Damn, Precious, you don't have to say no more. I've been wanting to feel what's mine for too long. I missed you, baby."

"I've missed you, too."

Precious and I made love and for that moment everything in the world seemed perfect. I was home with my wife and I finally had my life back.

Months went by and with each passing day, Precious and I ultimately found our happy medium as husband and wife. From the time we got married up until recently, we were on a never-ending roller coaster ride. As we relaxed by the pool, we enjoyed the serenity of being alone at our private estate without the outside chaos that seemed to prey on us ruthlessly.

"To think there was a time not too long ago that I believed we would never share moments like this again," Precious commented while sipping on some lemonade.

"I know it's important to never forget your past so you can appreciate the present and look forward to the future, but I don't want us wasting time dwelling on what Mike and Nico took away from us. Both of them tried to destroy us, but we survived. Mike is now behind bars where he belongs and Nico will soon follow unless death finds him first."

"You're right, but in regard to Nico—"

"What about him?"

"Supreme, when I thought you were dead, I died too. The only way I was able to keep my sanity was through my determination to get retribution for your murder. If it wasn't for that motivation, I would've crumbled up into a little ball and died."

"But we're both alive, baby, and that's all that matters," I said lovingly stroking the side of her bare leg.

"You're right, but I made a lot of mistakes when I thought you were dead. Some I wish I could take back, but I can't. I don't want you to hate me, but you have the right to know."

I put my finger over Precious's mouth. "Shhh, say no more, baby."

"But—"

"But nothing," I cut her off. "You don't have to explain anything to me. I can only imagine the hell you went through mentally and physically, believing I was dead. You did what you had to do to survive and you never have to explain to me what those things were because it wasn't your fault. It's called self-preservation, but now your man is home. You no longer have to survive because I'm here to take care of you. We've been blessed with another chance to get it right and we will. To our new beginning." I smiled, lifting up my glass.

"Speaking of new beginnings, do I look different to you?"

"Different how?" I questioned. "I mean with this sun shining down on your butterscotch skin, got you glistening in that red bikini. I would say you're looking even more sexy than usual... if that's even possible."

"Stop making me blush." Precious giggled, tossing one of her towels at me."

"It ain't my fault that my wife is bad as hell. What can I say, I married well."

"It's probably too soon for you to tell, but I'm noticing a little pouch in the front of my stomach and it ain't from me eating too many cupcakes either."

"I'm not following you... wait... I do think I'm following you. Are you saying what I think you're saying?"

"Yes! We're having a baby!!!!!" Precious jumped up and announced.

"My baby is having my baby." I stood up holding Precious tight.

"This time will be perfect, Supreme. I'm going to give you the child you deserve. You truly are the best thing that has ever happened to me."

"We're the best things that have ever happened to each other. I adore you... love for life."

Chapter Eighteen

Aaliyah

Three Years Later...

A nigga just can't catch a break... that was becoming my running theme. After all these years the drama continued to unfold like we were the stars of my mother's favorite soap opera The Young and the Restless. There was one major difference: that shit was made for TV and this shit was unfortunately our reality.

After the birth of our daughter, Aaliyah, we only seemed to have a limited amount of time to truly enjoy her because of Pretty Boy Mike and his equally sick sister, Maya. Not only was our daughter kidnapped, but now she was in the hospital fighting for her life after being in a terrible car accident. To see a child so small and delicate clinging on for her life was the sort of torture I wouldn't wish on my worst enemy. But just when I thought things couldn't get any worse, the never-ending storm known as my life continued to wreck havoc on me.

"At least Dr. Katz was able to stabilize her," Precious stated through her tears. "I know he said Aaliyah needs a blood transfusion to survive and the odds aren't in her favor due to her rare blood type, but she's a survivor like us. I know in my heart one of us is a match and all will be fine." I could tell Precious was trying to convince herself that, but it wasn't working. She was on the verge of having a nervous breakdown and if I didn't pull it together I would be joining her.

As we sat on the cold chairs in the emergency room, waiting for our names to be called so they could draw blood, a day that I prayed would never come had arrived. I couldn't help but reflect on the time I knew without a doubt our lives would never be the same again.

"Phil, I need you to take these samples and get a DNA test for me," I told my most trusted employee.

He eyed me suspiciously, but didn't dare question me. I wanted to put his mind at ease because his thoughts might've been much worse than the reality of the situation. I decided to tell him just enough to erase any unwanted suspicion.

"A few years ago, before I married Precious, I was seeing this woman. Recently, she got in touch with me saying she had a daughter and I was the father. She gave me a DNA sample to compare against mine."

"Boss, you don't owe me any explanations, but thank you. You've always seemed so committed to Precious so excuse me if I was a little shocked by the request. But this makes sense. As rich and famous as you are, I'm surprised more women haven't come forward trying to put their child off on you," Phil stated.

"Listen, it comes with the territory, but do me a favor, make sure you keep this under wraps. If she's my daughter of course I'll take care of her, but until I know for sure I want to keep this very low key."

"No problem, boss, and you know I'm always discreet, especially when it comes to your business."

"I appreciate the loyalty. Here's the address where to take the samples," I said, handing him a large envelope. "Make sure you have them put a rush on it."

"Will do." Phil nodded and walked out.

If I made Phil aware of the truth that the DNA test was for my daughter, Aaliyah, that would truly blow his mind. But for now no one needed to be aware of my suspicions, including my most trusted employee.

I locked myself in my office, fully aware that I would be pacing the floor until I got back the results of the DNA test. Even with the rush, the soonest I would have the results back was tomorrow and I doubted I would sleep the entire night. I began regretting even moving forward with the paternity test. Precious was my wife and she gave birth to Aaliyah while we were married so legally, whatever that DNA proved, in the court of law I was Aaliyah's father. But I couldn't let it go. I had to know.

I never forgot that day by the pool right before Precious told me she was pregnant. She began to make a confession and it had to do with Nico. I stopped her, but in my gut I had to wonder if she had concerns that he could be the father of the child she was carrying. I tried to shake off my doubts, but when Precious refused to cooperate with the police about Nico's involvement in her shooting, I couldn't let it go. She tried her best to convince me that she was in a good place in her life and wanted to put all that Nico stuff behind her. She begged me to respect her decision so I did, but it only further raised my concerns.

Knock... knock... knock...

"Baby, open the door," I heard Precious say, snapping me out of my thoughts. "You didn't hear me knocking... why did you have the door locked?"

"Sorry, babe. Phil must've locked it by accident when he left out." I then turned my attention to Aaliyah who Precious was holding in her arms. "Look at my beautiful baby girl." She was the only person in the world that brought a smile to my face every time I saw her. It didn't matter if I was having a good or bad day, Aaliyah made everything right.

"Look, she's reaching for you." Precious grinned. "She's such a daddy's girl."

"Yes, she is," I said, taking Aaliyah in my arms. She felt so warm, pure, and full of unconditional love. I held my baby and stared into her eyes. *She has to be mine, she just has to be,* I thought to myself never wanting to let Aaliyah go.

"Supreme! Didn't you hear me saying your name? They called us. It's time for them to take our blood," Precious informed me.

"You go 'head."

"Aren't you coming with me? They need your blood too. What the hell is wrong with you... why are you acting so strange and out of it? I know you're worried about Aaliyah, but so am I. I'm scared too."

"It's not that." My tone was low and reserved. I could see the frustration and confusion in Precious's face. She looked like she wanted to slap the shit out of me and I couldn't blame her. I was acting strange. I was struggling to get my thoughts together because they were all scrambled.

"Then what is it! Talk to me, Supreme. I don't need this shit right now. Our daughter could die so snap out of it."

"You're right, but it won't be me that can save her." Precious's eyes widened as if she wasn't following anything I was saying so I decided to just spit it out. "I'm not Aaliyah's biological father, Nico is."

Precious began to shake slightly. She leaned against the wall unable to keep her balance. Her world seemed to be crumbling around her, but there was nothing I could do to help.

"Supreme, they called our name. It's our turn." I shook my head when I heard Precious's voice. I realized that my mind was playing tricks on me. I hadn't revealed anything to my wife and I had no intention of doing so. I went ahead and took the test knowing that I wouldn't have the correct blood type. Precious was desperate to save our daughter and maybe that would compel her to admit Nico might be Aaliyah's father and possible match. There was also a good chance that Precious could be the match, but if Nico turned out to be the one who could save our daughter's life, then it worked out for the best that I didn't have him killed.

"I was beginning to think that you were avoiding me," my mother said while I sat at the bar stool in the kitchen watching her cook.

"Never that. I love you too much to avoid you." I smiled.

"Hum hmm. You might love me, but you

damn sure have been avoiding me. I can't blame you. When you first told me about Aaliyah, I was ready to call Precious every name in the book, but I've had plenty of time to let it all sink in so I'm a lot more calm now."

"Calm is good."

"But I'm still going to say, told you so," my mother quickly added.

"Told me so about what?"

"That Precious was gon' cause you nothing but problems. I still don't understand why you married her."

"Ma, please. Precious isn't perfect, but neither am I. I know I'm your son and you see no wrong in me, but I have my own skeletons and demons that I'm dealing with too. I have flaws; I'm just very good at camouflaging them unlike Precious. So stop being so hard on her."

"You gon' get tired of defending that woman. She knew there was a chance that Aaliyah was not your child and—"

"Stop right there. Aaliyah is my child. I still love her as if we share the same blood. That will never change."

"I didn't mean it like that, Supreme. Your father and me still love Aaliyah the exact same way too. She is our grandchild and that will never change. That doesn't negate the fact that

Precious should have been upfront with you from the start."

"She tried."

"Tried how? She clearly didn't try hard enough. That girl knew exactly what she was doing. Precious would much rather have an international superstar as the father of her child then some convicted drug dealer who left her for dead and murdered you all's unborn child. Now you're so attached to that baby just like we are that you're willing to forgive Precious and keep her as your wife. She's good at what she does... I'll give her credit for that," my mom snarled, whipping the mash potatoes aggressively.

"Are you forgetting that Precious thought I was dead? That was an extremely difficult time for her."

"So she decides to get back in bed with the man that tried to kill her and murdered her unborn child." My mom shook her head.

"I'm not saying I understand that either, but what I am saying is that Precious is my wife and we took vows. I'm committed to making our marriage work and being a father to Aaliyah. Anything else, I'll just take it day by day."

"Well good luck, son, because you're going to need it if you plan on staying married to that woman," my mom warned.

I knew my mom meant well and it was in her nature to speak her truth, but I had to live in mine. I knew a long time ago that Aaliyah wasn't my biological daughter, but that didn't change my love for Precious or Aaliyah. The one thing it did change was now that Nico knew the truth, the door was left wide open for him to be in our lives forever.

Chapter Nineteen

After The Love Is Gone

10 Years Later...

"Daddy, look at the picture I drew," Xavier said, holding up a drawing of racecars driving around a track.

"Impressive little man. You sure are talented," I said giving my son a hug.

"Daddy, hang it up on the wall with the rest

of my pictures," he said handing me the paper.

"Will do! Now you have time to draw one more picture and then we have to get ready to go to your grandparent's house. Okay?"

"Got you!" Xavier put his thumb up and headed back upstairs to his playroom.

"And where are you off to?" I questioned Aaliyah as we crossed paths headed to the kitchen.

"Justina is on her way over. We're going to hang out by the pool and listen to music."

"I guess that means you're not riding with me to drop off your brother."

"Where is he going... to the library to read a book?" Aaliyah joked. "I've never met a little kid that would rather read, draw, or study instead of playing video games." She shook her head.

"Be nice. He's your little brother."

"I know, Dad. So where are you taking him?"

"To your grandparent's house."

"Sounds fun, but ummm, tell Grandma and Grandpa I said hello. Maybe I'll catch them next time you drop the little brainiac off... cough... cough... excuse me, I mean, my brother. Talk to you later, Dad. Gotta go!" Aaliyah waved her hand disappearing upstairs to her bedroom.

As Aaliyah waved goodbye I couldn't help, but think how fast time flies. It seemed like yesterday I was rocking her to sleep in my arms, now she wanted to hang out by the pool with her best friend. Then there was Xavier, my little mini me, but the smart brainiac side as Aaliyah liked to call him. Xavier was born naturally smart and gifted just like I was, but I never had any interest in learning or schoolwork, but that was the exact opposite for Xavier. At such a young age, he already craved knowledge and that made me proud.

I glanced down at my watch to see what time it was before retrieving the car keys. As I was getting things together so we could leave, Precious came walking through the door.

"Where are you off to?" Precious questioned, giving me a kiss.

"I'm dropping Xavier off at my parent's house. You know it's his weekend to spend the night."

"He always looks forward to that. Is Aaliyah riding with you?"

"No, she's feeling too grown up for that. Actually, Justina is on her way over. They're gonna hang out by the pool. Can't blame them, it's beautiful out."

"What are you doing after you drop Xavier off? I was thinking maybe we could go out for dinner tonight, maybe do some dancing afterwards."

"Tonight isn't good for me. There's some business I need to handle."

"On a Saturday?" Precious gave me a quizzical look.

"Yes. It's a new venture I'm considering investing a substantial amount of money in."

"I see. If I didn't know better, I would think you were having an affair, Supreme. The last few months every time I suggest we do something together you come up with some excuse as to why you're too busy. Are you seeing someone?" my wife asked me point blank.

"No, I'm not, but I would be lying if I said I haven't thought about it," I admitted.

The color seemed to drain from Precious's face. I guess she wasn't expecting me to be so honest, but we were both too grown to be lying to each other.

"Is there a particular woman you've thought about having this affair with? Is there?!"

"Keep your voice down. I don't want the kids to hear you."

"Just answer the fuckin' question, Supreme."

"No, there isn't."

"Don't lie to me." Her eyes were now full of rage.

"Precious, if I wanted to lie, I wouldn't have admitted in the first place that I had thought about it."

"So why haven't you acted on it?"

"Because I still love you and I love our family."

"But you don't love me like you used to," Precious said with her voice cracking.

"It's not that."

"Then what?"

"You know what."

"Nico. I've told you so many times there is nothing going on between me and Nico, but it's like you don't believe me."

"You'll never admit it, but it's like you purposely give Nico false hope. I see the way you talk to him and interact with him. He's like a love sick puppy around you and you feed into that shit. I find it so fuckin' disrespectful. If the tables were turned and I acted like that with the mother of my child you would go ballistic."

"I don't know what you're talking about," Precious maintained.

"Of course that's what you'll say because like I said, you would never want to admit that shit. I bet you secretly hope that Nico never falls in love with another woman so he can forever have his tongue out wagging behind yo' ass. So yes, I still love you, but I guess the respect is slowly slipping away."

"Supreme, you don't mean that."

"I wouldn't have said it if I didn't." I could

hear what sounded like Xavier running down the stairs so I stopped talking.

"This conversation isn't over," Precious made clear.

"It is for now... there's my boy!" I said with enthusiasm not wanting Xavier to feel that anything was wrong when he ran up to me.

"I'm all ready to go, Daddy!"

"Xavier, you know you shouldn't be running in the house," Precious stated sternly.

"Sorry, Mommy."

"Come give me a hug." Xavier walked over and gave Precious a hug. "I know I can sound like a Grinch sometimes, but you know mommy loves you... right?'

"Yes!"

"You better." Precious smiled and started tickling Xavier until he laughed uncontrollably. These were the moments that I loved my wife more than anything and was determined to make the marriage work. But I would be lying if I didn't admit that sometimes it felt like the most difficult and impossible thing in the world."

"Are you ready, lil' man?"

"Yes, let's go! See you tomorrow, Mommy." Xavier gave Precious a kiss and headed towards the garage.

"I really do want us to finish our conversation," Precious said as I walked past her following behind Xavier.

"We will. I'll see you when I get back home."

I could tell that Precious expected me to give her a kiss goodbye, but honestly, my heart wasn't in it. Yes, there were moments that I was very much in love with my wife, but there were many more moments when I wondered if this marriage had run its course.

"T-Rock, I must say I was very surprised when you said you had a business proposition for me. We've always had a cordial relationship because our daughters are best friends, but us not so much," I said when I sat down to have dinner with Justina's father.

"No, we're not best friends, but I believe we have a mutual respect for each other even outside of the relationship our daughter's have. We've both been extremely successful in the music industry and continue to make big moves outside of it. I don't think it's a far stretch for us to collaborate on a business deal."

"Maybe, but why me? I'm sure you have other friends that are financially capable of going in on a business deal with you."

"I have a few and there is actually a third person in on the deal if you accept. But none of my friends have your name recognition. You're Supreme. To this day, you're still one of the most recognizable names in hip hop."

"Talk to me. Tell me about this business proposition," I said, leaning forward in my chair listening intently to what T-Roc had to say. From what I knew about T-Roc, I did respect his accomplishments and he seemed to be able to parlay his success to other things besides the music business. So he was right, there was a mutual respect there. If what he was talking about made financial sense then T-Roc could potentially have a new business partner.

On my drive back home, I thought about the conversation I had with T-Roc over dinner. His proposition was interesting, but I had reservations about the third investor. He was a silent partner that basically wanted to remain anonymous yet he would be the one putting up the initial money to launch the new business. It was costly, but if the idea T-Roc had worked, it would also be extremely profitable. The anonymous investor would make his money back triple times within the first few months. But I had serious reservations about doing business with someone I didn't know, but T-Roc did vouch for the anonymous investor. Plus, it wasn't costing me a penny to become a partner in what could end up being a very lucrative deal. I would sleep on it, but I thought tomorrow I'd place a phone call to T-Roc letting him know he could count me in.

Chapter 20

Is This The End

The Present...

I rested my head on the back of the sofa, staring up at the vaulted ceiling. My eyes continued to reflect up and then down at the fireplace while my mind drifted. This week had been full of reflecting and staying at this house wasn't helping. This was the estate in New Jersey that Precious and I had lived as husband and wife for many years. We shared so many wonderful memories and unfortunately a lot were bad.

We never sold this house even after Precious bought a place in New York City and I moved back to Beverly Hills. I guess neither one of us wanted to let it go. It was a source of so much history between us. We started our life here as husband and wife and we also ended it here. I remember like it was yesterday when I told Precious I wanted a divorce and moved out.

"Supreme, what are you doing? I know you're not packing up your stuff." Precious was hovering in my space and I really wanted her nowhere near me, but I tried to keep my cool.

"I'm packing up a few things. I'll be having someone else come by to get the rest of my belongings."

"Supreme, no! Please let's talk about this," Precious begged. "After the judge dismissed all the charges against Aaliyah you said a few words to her and then left the courthouse so fast. We haven't even had an opportunity to discuss everything."

"We have nothing to discuss. You admitted you've been having an affair with another man after T-Rock's wife called you out in open court. There's nothing left to say."

"I hate that happened, I really do," Precious said getting misty-eyed, but she was wasting her tears. "I was wrong, but marriages have survived affairs before."

"Not this marriage. We've been together a long time and neither of us has been perfect. But this, this is where I draw the line. I can't get over what you did and I don't want to. This marriage is done."

"I refuse to believe that. We have two beautiful kids that need us."

"I will always be there for both my kids, but Aaliyah is old enough to understand what is going on between us and I will spend all the time I can with Xavier. That's my son and he will always know that his father loves him."

"What about me?"

"What about you?" I shot back as I continued to pack some clothes.

"You can't be over me and our marriage just like that."

"That's where you're wrong, Precious. One thing you are right about is that there have been problems in our marriage for a very long time now. I've even thought about having my own affair, but I didn't act on it."

"I made a mistake, Supreme. It happens and I'm so sorry, but it's not worth throwing away our marriage. I want to fight for our love, not give up on it."

"You should've thought about that before you laid down with a man that wasn't your husband," I mocked. "My parents have been married for over forty years and I wanted that for us. But some things are so broken that they can't be fixed... that's this marriage. There's no fixing it. I tolerated the Nico situation because of my love for you and Aaliyah, but I don't have enough love left to give you a pass on your affair with Lorenzo."

"Supreme, please don't do this to me, to us. You're the love of my life."

"You used to be mine too, but not any more. I'll be in touch for us to discuss a visitation schedule with Xavier and I'll have my lawyers draw up the divorce papers so get yourself an attorney." I put the last item in my overnight bag, walked out that room and walked out my marriage.

Over the next few years I distanced myself from Precious. Eventually, she agreed to let Xavier come live with me in California and for the first time there was some real distance between us. But even after the divorce, our lives remained heavily intertwined. We endured many more obstacles, but we managed to get through them. Now we were facing yet another challenge, which brought a former business associate of mine, Arnez Douglass, back in the mix. So besides reflecting on my history with Precious, he was also heavy on my mind and it had to do with our daughter, Aaliyah.

Once Precious informed me that the man responsible for a great deal of tragedy in my life might be involved in the kidnapping of our missing daughter, I had to track Arnez down and pay him a visit. After my initial meeting with him, I was now counting down the days that Aaliyah was supposed to come home. Although Arnez would never admit it, my gut told me he knew a lot more about her disappearance than he was letting on. I was sure at this very moment he was plotting and scheming on doing whatever necessary to make sure he delivered on my demands. With the colorful history we shared, I was the last person Arnez wanted to gamble his life with.

I was so transfixed in thoughts of the past, the present and the future, that I barely heard my cell. I was somewhat reluctant to answer because I didn't recognize the number, but with all the drama going on I didn't want to take any chances.

"Hello."

"Dad, it's me Xavier."

"Whose phone are you calling me from?"

"Grandfather's. My battery died and I really needed to get in touch with you." I could hear panic in my son's voice.

"Xavier, what's going on?" I asked quickly, sitting up straight from my once relaxed position.

"It's Mom."

"What about her?"

"I think she's in trouble. Serious trouble."

"What kind of trouble?"

"The last time we talked to her she was following Maya. Grandfather tried to get her to stop, but you know Mom. When she gets something in her head there's no stopping her."

"What does she have in her head?"

"Aaliyah. She had grandfather call Maya and tell her that you were close to finding Aaliyah and that we should have her back by tomorrow."

"Why would Precious have Quentin do that?"

"Mom figured if Maya was behind the kidnapping she would go try and finish Aaliyah off because she wouldn't want her to tell us the truth."

"Damn! Precious should've left it alone. I had it all worked out," I unintentionally said out loud. "Where is your mother now?"

"Last we heard from her she was in Brooklyn. But we haven't been able to reach her and Maya isn't answering her phone either. Dad,

I'm worried. If Maya is responsible she's going to try to kill my mother and my sister."

"Xavier, calm down. I'm not going to let that happen. I've dealt with Maya before and so has your mother. Neither one of them are going to die if I have anything to do with it. I have to make some calls," I said grabbing my car keys. "I'll be in touch soon. If you hear from your mother, call me immediately."

"I will and Dad..."

"What is it, son?"

"Please find my mom and Aaliyah and bring them home," he pleaded.

"That's the plan son... that's the plan."

Immediately after hanging up with Xavier, I made my next call from my other phone, the untraceable one.

"What's up?" my connect answered.

"Stay right where you are. I'm on my way."

On my drive to the city, I was cursing Precious out the entire time. I was so fuckin' pissed that she could be so reckless. We both knew how dangerous Maya could be; especially when she felt her back was against the wall. For Precious to go in blindly not knowing for sure what she was up against was just stupid. If she would've told me what she was planning we could've done this shit together. Now I wasn't sure what was gonna happen. Only thing I knew for sure was that if anything happened to Precious or Aaliyah there would be hell to pay.

When I arrived at Sean's office, it brought back so many memories. He still resided in the same building that Platinum Records started at. Although it was no longer a record label, it was now a brand development and marketing firm.

"After not seeing you for years, I have now seen you twice in the last couple of weeks. Not saying I don't enjoy your company, but what gives." Sean laughed when I walked in his office.

"I'm here for the same reason as last time... Arnez."

"You know I do a lot of business with Arnez."

"Yeah a lot of illegal business," I reminded him.

"Whatever you want to call it. When you came to me last time, I gave you his whereabouts out of courtesy, respect, and our history. But I told you I wanted no parts of anything bad happening with Arnez. If he ever found out that I was the one that told you where he was, he would cut all business dealings with me and my pockets would take a major hit in return. So Supreme I can't help you."

"When I signed with Atomic Records, I gave you my share of Platinum. I didn't make you buy me out. I simply wanted the masters to my music and let you have everything else. We both know I didn't have to do that."

"True and you know how much I appreciated that. But the music business ain't what it used to be and that money is all but dried up," Sean explained.

"I get that and I also understand this new business you've been running doesn't bring in the sort of revenue that can keep you living the lifestyle that you have grown accustomed to. It's only to be expected you went right back and dived into a profession that's second nature to you. But while you're denying my request because you want to protect a man you do illegal drug activities with, there is something you should know."

"What's that?"

"Arnez is the reason your best friend and my mentor, J-Rock, is no longer here with us."

"Excuse me?" Sean came from behind his desk as if he needed to come closer to make sure he was hearing me correctly.

"You heard me. Arnez set that entire plan in motion. He was angry that I signed with Platinum without him being part of the deal. He had J-Rock killed and made it look like a robbery. He hoped that while I was mourning for J-Rock I would turn back to him for help. Of course that never happened."

"How long have you known all of this?"

"I found out a few months after it happened."

"Why didn't you tell me... why didn't you get retribution?"

"I got retribution in my own way," I said thinking back to the day I put a bullet in Rob's head, but Sean didn't need to know that. "I made Arnez leave New York. That's when he started his drug operation in Atlanta. The only reason I didn't kill Arnez was because he did play a critical role in the beginning part of my career so I threw him that one lifeline. But you don't owe him anything."

"I can't believe all this time I've been do-ing business with the man who took my broth-er away from me," Sean said sitting on the edge of his desk. He had his head down as if he was ashamed. Then he looked up at the ceiling. "J-Rock man, please forgive me. I never would've made money wit' that man if I knew he had your blood on his hands."

"Sean, I need that information from you. This is about my family and it's a matter of life or death. I need to find him right now. So tell me, where is Arnez?"

After leaving Sean's office, I rushed to Arnez's location. Time was of the essence and I didn't have much of it. Xavier hadn't called back so I knew that meant he still didn't hear from his mother. The only person who would know where Precious followed Maya to was Arnez. I was weaving through traffic and running lights as I made my way uptown. Arnez was staying at a townhouse in Harlem that Sean owned. He told me he had spoken to Arnez an hour ago and he was there. But Sean also gave me a key so I was getting in regardless.

When I went inside, I headed to the lower level since that was the unit Arnez was staying in. As I got close to the door, I could hear what sounded like two men yelling, but their voices were somewhat muffled so I couldn't understand what was being said. I waited outside the door for a few seconds to gauge how close to the door they were. The sound seemed to be coming from a slight distance so I thought it was safe for me to use the key to go inside without being detected.

I turned the doorknob slowly and peeped my head through the opening trying to get a view inside. Luckily, the door was well maintained so it didn't make any sort of sound as I cracked it open. The men continued arguing so I knew they were unaware of my presence. There was a long hallway that was dark and at the end I could see a bright light where the noise was coming from. I walked as quietly as I could with my back against the wall. When I got to the end of the hall I stopped and listened as I could now hear the two men clearly.

"Emory, put the gun away. You don't wanna do this," I could hear Arnez say now trying to use a calm tone. I guess he realized he wasn't getting anywhere with the loud boisterous voice.

"You've left me no choice, Arnez. Killing Aaliyah was never part of the plan. When her family finds out she's dead, none of us will be safe."

"You motherfuckin' right!" I barked, lodging the gun in the back of Emory's head. "Now give me this shit!" I continued, seizing Emory's weapon from his hand. I had caught him so off guard that he literally had no time to react. "Now go stand yo' punk ass over there by Arnez."

"Supreme, man, I'm so glad you here."

"You sound awfully relieved for a man that's 'bout to die," I stated.

"Why would you wanna kill me? I'm the one that's gonna bring Aaliyah home to you."

"How you gon' bring her home... in a body bag since you the one that killed her," Emory scoffed. I put my finger on the trigger and was about to end Arnez's life before he could say another word, but something made me hold back and not pull the trigger.

"Supreme, I need you to listen to me. I swear on everything, including my mother, that I did not kill your daughter or hurt her in any way." I had known Arnez for at least half of my life. He was a snake and a cold-blooded motherfucker, but I had grown to get a decent read on him. He definitely was involved with Aaliyah's disappearance, but I was leaning on the side of believing him when he said he didn't kill her.

"I know you don't know me, but this man is lying," Emory said pointing at Arnez. "He's full of shit. He killed your daughter and I know that for a fact!!" he stated in an absolute tone.

"Tell me how you're so sure." I could see Emory hesitating with his response. "If want to leave here alive you better tell me how you know Arnez killed my daughter."

Emory swallowed hard and bit down on his lip before speaking, "Maya told me."

"Maya!" Arnez howled. "How the fuck you

know Maya?"

"Yeah, how the fuck you know Maya?" I questioned just as curious to know as Arnez.

"We have a business and personal relationship," Emory admitted.

"You fuckin' Maya too?" Arnez asked with his face frowned up.

"What you mean, too? You fuckin' her?" Emory shot back.

"Of course I am. That trifling bitch! You mean to tell me she's been playing the two of us against each other all this time," Arnez said shaking his head in disgust. "She told you I killed Aaliyah?"

"Yes."

"When did Maya tell you that?" Arnez was pressed to know.

"Tonight. She called and told me tonight."

"Supreme," Arnez turned to me with desperation on his face. "Maya is lying. She must've told Emory that to turn him against me. You and I have a deal. We share a long history and you know I would never renege on any deal we make because I know what the consequences would be."

"Arnez, do you know where Maya is keeping Aaliyah?" I wanted to know.

"Yes. At a stash house in Brooklyn. I can take you there." I knew Arnez was telling the truth because Xavier told me that was where Precious was when he last spoke to her.

"Emory, do you know where that stash house is in Brooklyn?"

"No, Maya never told me about a stash house."

"Tell me exactly what Maya told you when you last spoke?"

"She told me that Arnez had killed Aaliyah so I needed to get rid of him because he was bringing too much heat on us. I agreed."

"That lying trifling bitch!" Arnez yelled out again. "She was setting me up to take the fall for everything."

"You need to chill, Arnez, and keep yo' voice down," I stated.

"So if you didn't kill Aaliyah that must mean Maya already did. I'm sorry I have to be the one to tell you that your daughter's dead." Emory took a long pause as the lurid levels of Maya's shenanigans were kicking in. "Maya killed Aaliyah. Oh my fuckin' goodness." He stood shaking his head.

"Oh my fuckin' goodness is right. I hope that pussy was worth your life 'cause that's what it cost you," I said, emptying three bullets in Emory. He fell back then we heard a heavy thump as his body hit the floor. Arnez stared down at Emory's dead body. He probably had flashbacks to that day when I killed his partner Rob.

"You did what you had to do," Arnez said halfheartedly.

"Take me to my daughter. For your sake she better be alive or you'll be a dead man too."

Bitch The Final Chapter Coming Soon…

A KING PRODUCTION
Bitch
The Final Chapter
Who Will Be Left Standing...
JOY DEJA KING

A KING PRODUCTION

Joy Deja King

Presents

So Hood So Rich

A NOVEL

Peter Mack

Chapter One

The tension in the air would hold a feather still in its thickness. The staid but venerable oak desks, occupied by sharply dressed professionals gleamed a tradition of defeat and misery under the glaring florescent lights.

No motion. Expectation pushed through the rich fabric of the dapper professionals. The lawyers occupying both desks on either side of the sterile expanse of courtroom watched with measured patience. Those pale long fingers of the judge sitting on high shuffled through the latest dismissal motion of the defendant. His skin stood in stark contrast; pale against the dark robe of final judgment. His thin neck reached out of the rich folds terrified at the vulnerability of being uncovered. Exposed. The steel gray eyes and shiny mop of silver hair were what conveyed his power and authority, even more so than his robe or the high copper base relief of the scales of justice hanging from the wall above his high backed chair.

BoDeen watched him intently. He noticed the low involuntary movement of his thin lips. White people intrigued him. The ones who had the power all looked the same to him. The spirit of authority pressed against their form giving them the same shape. Like an image illuminated when lightning strikes. The same sense of authority and surety. His college football coach. Pale. Slight. Sure. The detective that put him on death row. The silver shiny hair. The Warden at San Quentin. Those penetrating steel gray eyes. But this time he had one of them fighting for him. Not making him tackle. Not arresting him. Not locking him up. This time he was meeting them on their own turf with one of their own—though paid for handsomely enough—fighting for his freedom.

BoDeen watched the heavy gold Ivy League class ring move on the thin pale finger next to his thick, dark, scarred hand. He leaned closer. "Rubin, what's he doing?"

They both looked up at the judge, who was mumbling to himself, squinting at the notepad. His hawk eyes scanned the room above their heads. BoDeen knew without turning what Judge

Steinberg was surveying. The courtroom was full of shiny suits and pretty women. Hoodlums in stingy brim hats and gangsters in Khaki suits occupied a respectable number of rows. Coffee-, toffee-, vanilla-, and pecan-hued women with diamonds weighted in their ears and finely tailored clothes sheathing delicate limbs, sat pertly, protected by the ghetto security of the men they'd chosen to be their husbands, boyfriends, and baby daddies. All had a stake on the decision the Judge was about to make with BoDeen's life. Some privately wished he wouldn't be allowed to interrupt their hustle; others hoped he'd return them to former glory.

BoDeen could feel the heat from Missy's eyes burning across the distance. She held their son close. He'd grown since the last time BoDeen had seen him. Where Missy was vanilla-colored, their son, Dimp, was a deep mocha; his nine-year-old body was already forming into the sturdy sure shape of an athlete.

Dimp watched him from behind. His strong thick neck escaped the white shirt collar and his broad shoulders stretched the dark suit jacket. The light bounced off his bald shiny head. Dimp ran his own small fingers through his thick curls and wondered if his mom would let him cut his hair off like his father. When BoDeen turned suddenly to catch him looking, Dimp's eyes never wavered, but communicated a strength that made BoDeen smile, proudly.

The Judge cleared his throat for attention or annoyance. He looked from one table to the other. His penetrating gaze finally settled on BoDeen's lawyer, Mr. Rubin.

"I've considered the defense motion for dismissal at great length," Judge Steinberg began. "It seems the district attorney will agree that since the key witness in this case has expired—mysterious circumstances to be sure—this court can't go investigating every murder in this God-forsaken city." He looked at Mr. Rubin with an unspoken communication then continued. "There lacks here the key testimony to hold the defendant."

At this, BoDeen's ears were plugged up with the alternate shouts, cries, audible gasps, and rustling of jewelry and footsteps of the people behind him. He vaguely felt Mr. Rubin shake his hand and hug him around his big shoulders. The gravel in the pale hand on high moved to pound in slow motion: case dismissed.

After nine years on death row, the infamous BoDeen was free; the ex-Arizona state, all-star linebacker who blew his knee out at the NFL Combine. The man who came home and turned his popularity and charisma into a million dollar drug business. Cop killer. Free.

A King Production

ORDER FORM

Name:

Address:

City/State:

Zip:

QUANTITY	TITLES	PRICE	TOTAL
	Bitch	$15.00	
	Bitch Reloaded	$15.00	
	The Bitch Is Back	$15.00	
	Queen Bitch	$15.00	
	Last Bitch Standing	$15.00	
	Superstar	$15.00	
	Ride Wit' Me	$12.00	
	Ride Wit' Me Part 2	$15.00	
	Stackin' Paper	$15.00	
	Trife Life To Lavish	$15.00	
	Trife Life To Lavish II	$15.00	
	Stackin' Paper II	$15.00	
	Rich or Famous	$15.00	
	Rich or Famous Part 2	$15.00	
	Rich or Famous Part 3	$15.00	
	Bitch A New Beginning	$15.00	
	Mafia Princess Part 1	$15.00	
	Mafia Princess Part 2	$15.00	
	Mafia Princess Part 3	$15.00	
	Mafia Princess Part 4	$15.00	
	Mafia Princess Part 5	$15.00	
	Boss Bitch	$15.00	
	Baller Bitches Vol. 1	$15.00	
	Baller Bitches Vol. 2	$15.00	
	Baller Bitches Vol. 3	$15.00	
	Bad Bitch	$15.00	
	Still The Baddest Bitch	$15.00	
	Power	$15.00	
	Power Part 2	$15.00	
	Drake	$15.00	
	Drake Part 2	$15.00	
	Female Hustler	$15.00	
	Female Hustler Part 2	$15.00	
	Princess Fever "Birthday Bash"	$9.99	
	Nico Carter The Men Of The Bitch Series	$15.00	
	Bitch The Beginning Of The End	$15.00	
	Supreme...Men Of The Bitch Series	$15.00	

Shipping/Handling (Via Priority Mail) $6.50 1-2 Books, $8.95 3-4 Books add $1.95 for ea. Additional book.

Total: $_____**FORMS OF ACCEPTED PAYMENTS:** Certified or government issued checks and money Orders, all ma
in orders take 5-7 Business days to be delivered